The Thought of High Windows

The Thought of High Windows

Lynne Kositsky

Kids Can Press

This is a work of fiction and any resemblance of characters to persons living or
dead is purely coincidental.

Kids Can Press acknowledges the financial support of the Government of
Ontario, through the Ontario Media Development Corporation's Ontario Book
Initiative; the Ontario Arts Council; the Canada Council for the Arts; and the
Government of Canada, through the BPIDP, for our publishing activity.

Published in Canada by
Kids Can Press Ltd.
29 Birch Avenue
Toronto, ON M4V 1E2

Published in the U.S. by
Kids Can Press Ltd.
2250 Military Road
Tonawanda, NY 14150

www.kidscanpress.com

Edited by Charis Wahl
Designed by Julia Naimska

Excerpt from "High Windows" from COLLECTED POEMS by Philip Larkin.
Copyright © 1988, 1989 by the Estate of Philip Larkin. Reprinted by permission
of Farrar, Straus and Giroux, LLC.

Printed and bound in Canada

CM 04 0 9 8 7 6 5 4 3 2 1
CM PA 04 0 9 8 7 6 5 4 3 2 1

National Library of Canada Cataloguing in Publication Data

Kositsky, Lynne, 1947–
    The thought of high windows / Lynne Kositsky.

ISBN 1-55337-621-8 (bound).   ISBN 1-55337-622-6 (pbk.)

I. Title.

PS8571.O85T46 2004   jC813'.54   C2003-904814-4

Kids Can Press is a *COUS*™ Entertainment company

For Roger:

My dearest Elephant,
My far-away yet close companion,
My little brother,
My always friend.

Rather than words comes the thought of high windows:
The sun-comprehending glass,
And beyond it, the deep blue air, that shows
Nothing, and is nowhere, and is endless.

Philip Larkin

Chapter One

I jump out of windows.

I don't do it out of bravery or stupidity but with a kind of compulsion when things aren't going my way. Once it saved me, once it almost got me killed, but more of that later.

I've been jumping, or trying to, since I was tiny. My mama — I can't stop thinking of her all the time, though it makes me sad — told me that, once, while she was talking to a neighbor in the yard she saw me about to launch myself from a second-floor window. I was around eighteen months old and must have scrambled out of my crib. Apparently, I was belly down and already half over the sill.

"No, Esther!" she screamed.

She ran upstairs, her heart pounding, and managed to catch a corner of my smock as I wriggled out. Perhaps the neighbor stood underneath the window to catch me. Perhaps she walked away. Mama never told that part of the story, so I'm not sure.

Come to think of it, it's amazing how much you have to rely on other people for versions of your early life. I hardly remember anything before I was five, except the park, and the smell of new bread in our apartment and the bluish-red pattern of the living-room rug. And the snow. It cleansed my world each winter, drifting over the trees and grass, the roads and the sharp roofs of the city, leaving its icy calling card on our windowpanes. It also obliterated the swastikas like deformed spiders chalked on the pavement. I remember them, the swastikas. I just didn't know their power. But those swastikas are the reason I'm here now, standing outside a ramshackle barn next to a French castle.

The castle is huge. It glimmers in the noon sun as though it might melt. Mountains, almost transparent with heat, are ranged behind it. This is France, the south of France, and like the Israelites wandering in the desert, about sixty of us Jewish kids have arrived here after what seems like forty years. First we traveled to Belgium by train when the Nazis started persecuting the Jews in Germany, thinking we would make a home there; but after they invaded Brussels, our Red Cross directors packed us into cattle cars and brought us here. If Belgium seemed like the promised land, flowing with milk and honey — or at least half-decent food — France is strange, brooding, a giant and alien presence pressing down on all us outcasts. The war has begun. The second great war. You'd think that would make us friends, comrades in arms, because we're all escapees; but until about three days ago we'd been fighting our own dirty little war. I always seemed to get the worst of it.

That's partly because I'm fat, but mostly because I'm what the other girls call "Old Jewish." They say it snottily, tossing their heads. That means I lived in the Jewish quarter, ate *knaidlech* and *lokshen,* went to *shul* and listened to my parents speak to each other in Yiddish, even though they talked to my little brother and me in German. To the girls, being Old Jewish is shameful, as if I deserve to be persecuted by Hitler.

Of course, they don't deserve to be persecuted at all. They just can't understand what's happening — or why it's happening to *them*. They're new, modern Jews. They lived in apartments in the gentile part of town, ate gentile food, dressed like gentiles, spoke only German. Some even celebrated Christmas. They thought they'd crossed over. They thought they were safe. Their problem is that Hitler disagreed, and to their minds it's Jews like me that made Hitler hate us all.

"We don't get the castle. We get to sleep in the barn." This is Rose, one of the counselors, her face creased with exhaustion.

"The barn. And we're supposed to live there." Eva, my number-one enemy, isn't asking a question. She is making an observation. Wrinkling her tiny nose with disgust, she raises her hands defensively against the open door as if it's an enormous mouth intent on swallowing her. Eva is petite and pretty, with china-blue eyes and blond curly hair. She looks so Aryan I can almost imagine her in the Hitler youth. A tiny bead of perspiration (Eva doesn't sweat) runs down her nose, and she wipes it away daintily. She is not speaking to me so I don't respond. Eva despises anyone who is plain or lumpy. Since I am both, she usually ignores me but calls me "the baker's fat daughter" when she calls me anything at all.

I glance inside. Our new home is a filthy, cobwebby building, dirty straw strewn across the floor. No furniture, not so much as a chair. Much as I dislike her, Eva is right for once. The barn looks horrible, smells of decay and mold. Why has the Red Cross brought us here, of all places?

"Come on." Heinz, a tall boy with bright orange hair motions us inside. "If we go in perhaps they'll feed us. I'm starving."

"And it can't be worse than what we've already been through," says Inge. She strides in, sits on the filthy floor, leans her back against the dirty gray wall and crosses her legs. Pulling her skirt down over her knees, she grins at all of us.

Inge is my heroine, even though she's New Jewish and dresses and speaks like the others. I can't help admiring her. She wasn't supposed to be with us, but she can outwit or outtalk anybody. When we got to the station in Belgium months ago, her name wasn't on any Red Cross list. She'd simply got on the train and stayed there. A black-coated woman, who seemed to be in charge, wanted to send her back to Germany. Inge straightened her back and said very solemnly, "I can't be sent back. I have nowhere to be sent back *to.*"

Her little suitcase appeared quite bereft, standing in the middle of the platform while ours were piled on buses, and she looked very vulnerable, which she really is not.

Everyone was looking at her — the chaperones, the other girls in our group, the station workers — but she just stared ahead defiantly as the rain soaked us.

"Everybody comes from somewhere, mademoiselle, so you might as well give us your address." The woman in the black coat clicked her teeth with impatience.

"I've forgotten. The long journey has exhausted it

out of me, but I'll be glad to go wherever the other girls are going."

"Tell me where you come from, mademoiselle, if you'd be so kind. We can't stand here in the pouring rain all day."

Inge gave her a wide, glittering smile but said nothing, wouldn't tell her name or show her passport; so in the end, the woman gave up and put her in the children's home with the rest of us. Inge hadn't gone through the process — hadn't asked the Cultural Society to help her leave Germany, didn't have the right papers. She wasn't even wearing the little red tag we'd all been given to show we belonged to the group. I'd have been sent back to Berlin in a minute, but Inge has some magical quality. I can't define it — I just know I don't have it. Yet she's the only girl who is passably kind to me.

Greta is speaking, pulling me back to the present. "Look at that castle. A château, they call it. Looks like something out of Transylvania. Whew! Six days crammed in a boxcar with too many clothes on, a bomb, that little village of falling-down houses, that horrible man with the stinking coat who shouted at us all the way down the road — just to get to this scabby barn next to a vampire castle. I think I need a rest." She pushes back her dark hair, which is so lank and greasy it's sticking together, and goes to sit by Inge. They've never been really friendly. Maybe the old enmities are breaking down a bit, I think hopefully. No one has been particularly nasty to me for at least three days, not since our train was bombed. The last car was a charred ruin. People were killed. Death can happen to anyone, and fast. That terrifies me. It's horrible to think that my good luck might arise from the tragedy of others, but since that happened I find myself breathing a bit easier.

Others are pushing by me: Werner, Karl, Manfred, Naomi, and Lisel. Eva follows reluctantly, picking through the straw with her delicate feet as though it might rear up and bite her. Walter, my best friend — well, actually, my only friend — is still standing on the threshold. He whispers a few words in Eva's ear as she enters. I can't catch what he's saying, but even though she ducks away, sticks her nose in the air and doesn't respond, I feel almost crushed by envy. "Fool," I whisper. Myself or him? Maybe both. My feelings are too confused to sort out.

A crowd of littler children and counselors come tramping over the hill and follow the older boys and girls inside. Our directeur and directrice from the Belgian children's homes are last. Walter and I remain standing in the heat. A threadbare peaked cap, slung low over his forehead, hides his eyes. His mouth, though, is visible, turned down, sulky. He doesn't say a word, just stands there, kicking at the path till clouds of dirt permeate the rusty, burning air.

I shift from foot to foot, put down my suitcase, which is making my arm ache. I wish I had muscles, but I'm weak. Naomi says that's because I ate too many Yiddish cookies. I know that's not true. I had lots of strength in Berlin — I used to hoist myself onto the roof — but the food they gave us at the orphanage has drained it out of me.

Although I don't want to look as though I'm waiting for Walter, I am, because there's a void in me if I move too far away. It's as if I'm tied to him with invisible elastic. I can't go inside without him. "Are you coming?" I ask at last, as casually as I can. I'm trying to look as though I'm not really there, but it's hard because I'm so huge.

He doesn't respond.

"I'm sorry. Are you upset because Eva didn't answer you? She's like that to most people, not just you."

"What do you know, Mouse?" His nickname for me.

"More than you think."

He leaps forward so suddenly that I recoil. Scooping up his case, leaving mine on the path, he strides into the barn. His eyes glitter like brilliant yellow stones, cold and sharp and hard, and I want to kick myself for speaking out, for having made him angry with me. Walter is often angry, though. I accept that in him and shrug. It's part of the cost of being his friend.

Chapter Two

It's evening at last. I go over everything in my mind, everything since we left Germany, months and months ago. There is a sour taste in my mouth, but I force myself to push back into the past, if only to try to figure out why I can't do anything right, even with Walter. I spend a lot of time in the past — now I try to relive my first sighting of him at the children's home in Belgium. The girls and the boys lived in separate orphanages there, but we had a party to get introduced before we started school together. I felt more alone than ever as first two boys, then three, then a few girls crossed the great divide of the dining hall to congregate in the middle. The hall was enormous with all its chairs and tables cleared away. I didn't dare walk across that vast space, propping myself against a wall instead. Everyone seemed to be talking and laughing — everyone except me.

No, that's not true. There was one boy as silent as I was. About two years older than me, I guessed, with straight, tawny hair that fell across his forehead and a bony stoop as if he hadn't quite grown into his body. He skulked around the edges of the celebration, scowling at the revelers, until suddenly he was standing close to me. I didn't like his angry amber eyes, the curve of his upper lip, but couldn't help feeling a strange comradeship, kinship almost — probably because we were both alone and gloomy. A scrap of paper crammed with Hebrew writing fell from his pocket. He picked it up with a snort, scrunched it in his hand.

"*Gott im Himmel,*" I heard him mutter, as he looked around, God in heaven, even though we weren't supposed to speak German, only the French we were learning with such difficulty. But the supervisors were on the other side of the hall, and everyone broke the language rule with a studied carelessness when they could. It went too much against nature to speak all the time in a foreign tongue, with its soft dark syllables.

"Shut up, Walter," one of the boys hissed. "Relax. Enjoy yourself for once."

Walter glowered, stared down his straight, narrow nose at the floor. *Gott im Himmel,* I found myself repeating, wrapping my tongue around the words, imitating his tone. He looked German, with his light hair and eyes and arrogant mouth, but there was something about him that reminded me suddenly of Yossi, a grinning yeshiva boy who had lived on our street in Berlin, although they look nothing alike and Walter hardly ever grins. I wanted to risk everything that evening, move across the small space that separated us and talk to him. I wanted to smile because we were so different yet so similar — he must be Old Jewish, too. But I didn't have the courage to speak to him, and soon he went back to the boys' orphanage with the others.

Since then, of course, I've become friends with him. Or allowed him to befriend me. Or imagined we are friends. Can anyone really be friends with Walter? He's so unpredictable, so somewhere *else,* most of the time. Come to think of it, why would anyone be friends with *me?* I'm unattractive and unclever. He calls me Mouse because I once made a stupid mistake in French translation back in Belgium. That's a long story.

All this thinking hasn't helped — I still don't understand anything. Listening to the crickets' fitful song, I fall asleep on the scratchy hay.

Chapter Three

We've been here two weeks, and every day is worse than the last — much worse than in Belgium. I've developed horrid, pus-filled blisters in my mouth that burn when I eat, and painful sores on my legs. Now my head is itching like crazy, too. There's blood under my fingernails when I awake one morning — I must have scratched my head raw during the night. There's no longer any way to avoid seeing Rose, who looks after our medical needs.

"You've got head lice. Almost everyone has them in this filthy barn. Pah." She goes over to a table and picks up a comb saturated with kerosene. Dust flies off the tabletop. A pungent, chemical smell makes me choke.

"There's no other way," she says, fetching a pair of scissors and a razor after combing through my hair several times. "Your head is so badly infested I'm going to have to shave it."

"*No!*"

"Come on, Esther. You're not the only one. Most of the girls will have to be clipped or shaved. It's this awful place, God help us." She crosses herself with the scissors.

"No!" I screech again, flinging my hands up to protect my hair. I can still hear the softness in Walter's voice when he once spoke of all the light brown hair falling around my face. He hugged me another time he talked of it and made me laugh, saying I looked more like a bunny than a mouse, a little round bunny with a button nose. I once had a book called *Button Nose, the Puppy* that my mother had made for me. The puppy had a real gray button where his nose should have been. Mama used to read the book to me and I turned over the fabric pages. I was really small, and she cuddled me when she finished and tucked me into bed. I still need to be hugged. Mama's not here, and Walter, who can be affectionate when he wants to be, won't ever hug me again if I'm bald. Rose just doesn't understand.

"All right, we'll leave it for now," she says at last. "But you'll be sorry and cause me a lot more grief in the long run. Come back if … no, *when* it gets worse."

It does get worse but I don't go back. I will myself not to scratch as I go about my work, helping cook the horrible turnip soup that is almost our only food, building a bonfire to heat water to wash ourselves and clean our filthy clothes. They're piled in heaps, as there are no cupboards. No one ever changes the straw on the floor, and I blame it for my lice. But the itching crescendos into such revolting pain that I can't concentrate on anything. I'm sure I can actually feel the horrid creatures dancing on my head, their microscopic louse boots banging on my brain. When I sleep, if I sleep, I dream of bugs doing American square dances:

Swing your partner
As we go
Side to side
And do-si-do.

One day breakfast is more awful than usual. There is a white worm spiraling in my soup. I all but vomit at its fleshy, revolting segments, its slow circular movement in the bowl, but I have only a few minutes to eat. I gag down the soup, avoiding the worm, which I can't bear to fish out, but something snaps in me. The barn smells of sweaty turnips, long-gone horses, and diapers, and the bugs are still dancing on my head — even my arms and legs itch madly. I begin to moan, scratching my scalp until clots of blood and torn-out hair clog my fingernails. "Where's Mama?" I wonder. "She'd fix this. She'd give me chicken soup and chopped liver." The absurdity almost makes me giggle. Inge finds me in a corner.

"You crying or laughing?"

I'm not sure.

"Come on." She grins. "We've all been through it." She drags me to Rose, and I smell the horrible stink of kerosene. The other girls have had their hair cut very short, but I have to be shaved. Afterwards, Rose hands me a mirror. Inge is biting at her top lip as if to stop herself from crying out. You'd think it was her being shaved, not me.

"See," Rose barks at me, without a tinge of sympathy. "Look what happens when you won't do as you're told."

I stare at my reflection. The lice have burrowed into my scalp, and my head's a mass of bloody sores. I wince. Before, I was plain. Now I'm grotesque. I can't bear to look at myself. Inge can't either, apparently. She is carefully examining the wooden beams that support the roof.

Applying some greasy medicine that smells like pork fat, Rose tells me sternly not to scratch.

"You don't need to worry."

"I'm not worried. I'm just very, very tired." She goes back to the kitchen area.

It's evening at last. "Poor Mouse." Walter smiles sadly at my bald head, its helmet of ointment shining like a beacon. "Never mind. You'll heal up nicely and your lovely brown mouse fur will soon grow back." It's the first time he's spoken to me in days. It's almost worth losing my hair for.

"What are you doing?" I ask. There's a piece of paper on his lap crammed with numbers and Hebrew and Greek letters.

"The number of the beast is six sixty-six." His speech is clipped, urgent. He has straw in his hair, which, unfairly, is almost as long as a girl's.

I shake my head.

"One of the villagers gave me a Bible. Trying to convert me, I expect. The book of Revelation, in the New Testament, says: 'Those who understand should count the number of the beast, for it is the number of a person, and its number is six sixty-six.' I'm trying to find a way to get the letters in Hitler's name to add up to that. Then we'll be able to beat him."

"Have you succeeded yet?"

"Are you making fun of me?" His eyes narrow. Like me, Walter hates being made fun of.

"No, of course not," I say, although maybe I was, a little bit. "I'm just stupid, I guess — don't know the right questions to ask."

"Well, of course I haven't succeeded, Mouse. Look here. All the letters have corresponding numbers in Hebrew and Greek. *H* is eight, *I* is nine, *T* is two hundred, *L* is thirty, *E* is five, *R* is ninety. What does that add up to?"

I think for a minute, or try to. My brain is blank. Walter is talking to me — the Mouse part of me is ecstatic.

"Three hundred and forty-two," Walter interjects impatiently. "I'm still more than three hundred short. That's what I'm working on, finding various permutations of his first name. Now do you get it?"

I smile knowledgeably. But actually I can't figure out how Hitler's name adding up to six sixty-six will defeat him. I'm also uneasy talking about the New Testament — we're *Jewish,* after all. But I sweat when anyone mentions numerology, gematria or Kabbalah, the mystical fringes of Judaism that my father, although a scholar as a youth, always avoided. They are too dangerous, they could call down the wrath of God on us. Numbers seem innocuous, just small squiggles on the page, but put together in certain ways they can be deadly, they weave nets of spells and can capture you in them. They're definitely off limits to me. I believe they should be off limits to Walter, too, and tell him so.

"Mouse, cease," he says crossly. "There's an order to ending this Hitler problem, just like there's an order to everything, and I'm going to find it."

I snarl inwardly but shut up. Soon he's back working, a puzzled expression on his face.

"It's bad luck," I want to say, "and really stupid, looking for trouble." But instead I ask, surprising myself: "How's it going with Eva? Is she being a bit kinder?"

I hope he's going to say he doesn't know what I'm talking about, but instead he glances up, speculatively, if reluctantly. I can see he wants to be busy with his numbers. "It's going very well, I think. I brought her some flowers and berries in my cap, and she thanked me very prettily for them. She's a nice girl, Mouse, and brilliant too. She understands everything I tell her."

Eva, brilliant? Walter really has it bad. But so do I. I can't even feel my head itching because I'm on fire with envy. I can't stand to be near him another minute — he's impossible, he doesn't understand how much he hurts me. I must be driving him mad, too, because he picks up his papers and ambles away, his walk loose, uncoordinated, as if God dropped a few stitches knitting him together.

My stupid eyes are burning. I throw a quick goodnight at his back and rush off to my little box of a bed that's been hastily thrown together by the counselors and older boys. We all have beds now, beds and stools, rickety though they are. Walter might be a whiz at gematria, he might understand the magic of numbers, but he and the others are miserable failures at carpentry. If I sleep on my left side, the way I'm most comfortable, the bed collapses. That could be funny if it wasn't so pathetic.

Something catches my eye, and I glance through the barn window. There's a light on in the castle, and I imagine the moths dancing around it. Only one light in only one room because there's only one occupant — someone lonelier and crazier than I am. Our directrice, who's been over to speak to him and bargain for eggs, says the castle is disgusting, decrepit, full of cobwebs and rats, but I still think we'd be better off there. All that space for one sorry-faced man. And only this barn for all of us. It doesn't make sense.

My scalp starts to itch again. Pulling my blanket over my head with a groan, I scratch desperately, relishing the sharp, stinging pain. It's an effective, if dangerous, diversion. "You'll get an infection in your brain and it'll kill you," I hear Mama say. At first I block her out because I really, really don't care. But then I let the memories fly in like huge birds, soaring through the giant window of the past.

Chapter Four

The shadows on the barn wall speak to me as if they're my mama, my papa, my little brother, Josef. My old home in the Jewish quarter of Berlin returns to me with all its smells and sounds, familiar yet disturbing. Going to school meant crossing into the other world, into gentile German territory. I can still trace my way there, and now I want to, want to bring it all back. Some of it, particularly the end-time, is dreadful, but almost anything is preferable to the lonely and dislocated now.

I walked slowly — too slowly — to school, because I hated arriving, was always in trouble. I forgot my homework, fought with the other girls, couldn't keep my mouth shut. We lived above Papa's bakery, so I'd come out the store door and dawdle past the fish shop with its barrels of schmaltz and pickled herrings, past the cramped grocery with its beguiling perfume of prunes, dried apples and raisins, until I reached the shoemaker's at the end of the street. Even this early in the morning, I could hear the tap, tap of his little hammer, the sadness of his Yiddish song. I don't speak much Yiddish, but Mama and Papa spoke it to each other and I recognized its soft familiar cadences. I cling to the sound. Now we must appear as un-Jewish as possible so as not to alarm people, and I've not heard more than ten words of Yiddish since leaving home. Only Walter speaks it, just as he writes gematria, rejoicing in the power, the danger of otherness.

The boys from the yeshiva, the Jewish boys' school, usually congregated at the corner. They gabbled on in Yiddish, too, their earlocks bobbing, but they quieted and lowered their eyes as I went by.

That boy, Yossi, flies through the window of the past. He lands in the forefront of my mind: small and lithe, darting in and out among the young men. His mouth is full of bagel, his grinning monkey face mobile as his lips open to speak or tear off another piece of bread. Yossi. Where is he? Is he alive? I drown the thought.

"Have you remembered your breakfast box?" Mama would yell from the window above the bakery. Yossi and the other boys would stare up at her big curly head, her round pink face, and giggle.

"Yes, Mama," I'd mumble, making a face.

"Check and see, Esther-leh. I packed you two egg sandwiches and an apple."

"The box is right here in my hand, and it's full, I can tell." Hitching my brown haversack a little higher on my shoulders, I'd scuttle around the corner, anxious to get away from her cloying, fussy motherliness. But even as I did, I felt the need to return. There was always that horrible moment when I turned into Grindeer Street, five minutes from our apartment — as soon as I saw the kosher butcher's with its crates of squawking chickens waiting for the Sabbath — my heart would plummet. I was committed now — the picture of Adolf Hitler on the classroom wall, the teasing and whispers of the students, the punishments of the teachers. I had passed the safety marker between *us* and *them*, the Jews and the Germans, and I felt like a caged hen myself, dreading the chop.

It would be hours before I could rush back to the haven of my family and slam the door on all the bad happenings of the morning. Mama didn't embarrass me then. She was plump and welcoming, her apron warm — smelling of the carp, *lokshen* soup and yeast buns she was preparing for dinner. She could have fetched the buns from our bakery but took pride in making them herself. It was almost as if she was saying: see, I'm the mama. I know how to take care of my family, to keep us safe inside a wall of nourishment.

Sometimes I cried when I got home.

"Don't, Esther," Papa would say as he came up for lunch. He hated my distress so much he would almost cry himself. "You're so beautiful and clever. How can you not be doing well at school?"

"Beautiful, huh. I'm big and lumpy. The girls say it's all the Jewish food I eat. And even if I was clever, which I'm not, intelligence doesn't count. Only being gentile does."

Papa would shake his graying head and turn back to his soup, spooning it up as fast as he could so he could get back to the store. Mama was more practical. "Go do your homework, then play with your little brother. He misses you when you're gone."

I'd stuff a piece of buttered bread and cheese into my mouth and disappear into the dark bedroom we all shared, opening the window and looking out over the tangle of tiny backyards and narrow streets. Far off, away from the Jewish district, I could just see the curved border of my favorite park, picture the sharp-toothed leaves, pink buds and enormous yellow flowers. Sometimes, to view it better, I hung over the window ledge. Too often, when the room was very oppressive and I was feeling particularly sad or disagreeable, I climbed onto the sill, dug my feet into indentations in the outside wall, and used my hands as grappling hooks to swing up to the roof. I was strong then, and it was safer to heave myself up than to launch myself down. Mama would have had a fit, though, if she'd seen me treating anyone on the street below to a view of my much-faded school knickers.

But she never caught me, and I sat on the roof slates for many precious minutes, sometimes even an hour if I knew she was cooking a complicated dish or waxing the floorboards around the rug. Up there, I owned the city. Everything nasty was more remote than it was in regular life, less annoying, diminished. And everything good was there to dream on. As time went by, I stayed longer and longer on my perch, imagining myself walking over the park grass, smelling the geraniums, devising torture for the girls and teachers at school. It was my happiest place. But it's also where I first spied brown-shirted youths, swastikas on their arms.

Herr Goldmark, who owned the bakery two streets up and was our good-natured competitor, had been putting out poppy-seed rolls when the brownshirts rolled past. Now he was holding his head as blood streamed through his fingers. A few of the yeshiva boys had been in his store shopping for lunch. Hats knocked off, fringes flying, they were suddenly racing home through the scrubby back-yards, fanning out from the warm hub of the bakery to a dozen streets.

Yossi was the last out of the store, clutching his half-eaten bagel. One vicious punch and he was down. Even now I hear him groan, feel his long mournful cry reverberate against my breastbone, and I moan secretly in reply. His attacker leaned over. Taking a knife from his pocket he cut off one of Yossi's side-curls and flourished it before dropping the fluffy skein of hair and careening down the pavement. Pulling himself up painfully, Yossi crept along the street. For a moment, he stares straight at me through time. His face is lopsided without its earlock, sad, wizened.

I can't stand any more. "Go away," I whisper. "Go away." I face the wall and try to sleep.

In the morning I receive a letter from Mama, a miracle in this place.

"Fraülein Lumpy has a letter from home, littered with spelling mistakes, no doubt, from her blessed frumpy mother," drawls Naomi. She holds the precious letter aloft before tossing it onto my bed.

"My mother is not frumpy. She's beautiful. You don't even know her!"

"So, is it your father who's the frump?" asks Eva, running her eyes over me so pointedly that the other girls laugh.

"You're just jealous I got a letter." I am unhurtable, triumphant. I have a link with my own, old life. Even the blue paper is familiar. The message itself is disappointing, full of the usual warnings and admonitions to dress properly, speak nicely and eat well, as if I have any choice.

But it's still a letter, a tiny silken filament that stretches from her to me. And it says "love from Mama" at the end. We are still joined. I am still the child of my family.

Much, much later I notice the postmark. Forwarded from the children's home in Belgium, the letter was mailed from Berlin just one week after I left Germany. It is as stale as year-old bread.

Chapter Five

Walter seeks me out while I'm trying to wash a few clothes. He saunters right up to me.

"Mouse," he says warmly.

"Yes?" I wring out a blouse and spread it over a rock.

"Could you do me a favor?"

I look around. We're entirely alone. He holds out an envelope. I wipe my wet hands on my skirt to receive it, but don't quite dare. *Something for me. Something he wants me to look at.*

I stare up at him questioningly. His eyes flash hazel, bluish green and finally that dark amber I love. His face is set in harsh downward lines — I guess it's really shyness. He masks anything that makes him seem vulnerable. I feel anxious, then sorry for him. But my heart is singing because suddenly I wonder if he feels nervous because of me. I'm the one he always speaks to. I'm his best friend.

"You don't have to feel shy if you want to show me something or … admit something to me," I say hopefully.

"Don't be stupid, Mouse. Of course I'm not shy." He pauses, his eyes hooded, and stares at me suspiciously. My head itches and I scratch.

"Don't do that. You're making it bleed again."

"Sorry." My hands snake behind my back and I clasp

them tightly. My hair is growing in and it feels like sand-paper, like a million little daggers pressing through the scalp.

"Listen, Mouse, can I trust you with a secret?"

I nod. "Of course."

"Well, there's a girl here I *am* shy of — she's too beautiful for words. I want to give her this, but haven't the courage. Could you pass it along for me?"

I should have guessed. Stupid, stupid Mouse. I take the envelope and turn it over. *Eva,* in bold black strokes that swerve upwards from left to right. *Eva Zilber.* I feel as if I've been smashed in the face, want to rip the disgusting thing into a hundred tiny pieces. But I stuff it in my pocket, Walter leaves, and I go on with my washing.

Later, I walk away from the barn and take the letter out with a thrill of guilt. I didn't refuse. I was too shocked. But I also didn't promise him anything. For a moment, I wish that both he and Eva would tumble into a deep dark hole and stay there forever.

It's a beautiful day, the river glistening, the woods shimmering with glossy pastel flowers. But I have no time to appreciate the landscape. I carefully unstick the envelope flap and pull out the flimsy sheet of paper. I hesitate for a moment. This is *wrong*. But then I inhale the words, sucking them into my brain as though they're meant for me.

I really like you a lot. Will you come out walking Sunday afternoon? Walter.

I scrunch up the note and throw it on the pebbly ground. I stamp on it several times for good measure, gasping deeply to stop myself from screaming out my rage.

I'm about to tear the envelope to shreds — want to feel the satisfaction of the tiny mangled bits between my fingers — but what if Walter asks me for Eva's reply? I can't see myself hanging my head like a naughty child and admitting the truth, but I don't want to lie to him, either. So, what if I actually take the note to Eva? I know what she'll do. She'll laugh. It'll serve Walter right. Then maybe, just maybe, he'll realize what bitches some girls are and value me the more.

Not that I ever, ever want to be his friend again. I've lost all sympathy, all liking for him. I pick up the note, do my best to smooth it out. I dust my bootprints off it and fold it back in the envelope. Lonelier than I've ever felt, I meander by the river until dusk floats along the water and into my soul. Creeping at last into the girls' part of the barn, which is empty, I walk heavily over to Eva's bed and drop the envelope on it.

Chapter Six

"Girls, you'll never guess," crows Eva.

"What is it?"

"Let's hear."

"Do tell."

"I have a letter from the lean, mean Walter. It's a bit rumpled, rather like the creature himself. Ooh la la! However did it get here?"

"He probably cast a spell on some minion so she'd deliver it," says Greta, staring at me. "What does it say?"

"*I really like you a lot.*' How delicious. '*Will you come out walking Sunday afternoon?*' And how formal. I wonder if I should reply."

"Yes, yes, yes," chorus her friends.

Eva takes up pencil and paper. "Dear Walter," she begins, practicing possibilities. "It has come to my attention that you would like me to go out with you on Sunday next."

"Much as I should like to ..." chimes in Naomi.

"Good," says Eva. "Go on."

"... young ladies living at the barn are unfortunately unable to venture out with young men unaccompanied," Greta continues with a giggle.

"However, I shall keep your letter close to my bosom ..." Eva positively shrieks.

"Are you sure?" Naomi sounds doubtful.

"Yes. Oh, yes." Eva is now scribbling it all down, the pencil making a horrid scratching sound as it bounces across the page. She licks the lead. Two bright crimson spots blaze on her cheeks. "And I shall hope with a deep and passionate fervor that we might become closer as time goes on. Fondly yours, Eva Zilber. There, brilliant. Now why are you glaring at me, Esther Navy Knickers?"

"I'm not glaring at you. I'm not even looking at you. I have no interest in either you or Walter."

"Then you won't mind delivering this, will you?" Eva certainly knows how to dig the knife in.

"Not at all. I'll give it to him tomorrow."

I feel a sad affection for Walter, a desperate sympathy all over again. When everyone's asleep, I do what I should have done with the first note, rip it into a thousand little pieces. Then I stuff the telltale bits into my shoe till I can get rid of them. Walter will never have the courage to ask Eva anything about his stupid letter, so I'm safe.

For once, sleep comes easily.

Chapter Seven

"Did you give it to her?" Walter asks a few days later, as we stand outside the barn. He's wearing that hat again.

"Give what to who?" I ask, stalling for time. It's better he shouldn't know anything of what happened, but I feel cornered, don't know how to reply to him.

"You never did give her the note, did you? You never gave Eva what I wrote. Now she'll never, never like me, and it's all your fault." He speaks so savagely, his lips twisted into such a snarl, that I shrink back against the wall of the barn. There is a smell of ancient wood, of people long dead.

"You asked me to give it to Eva, and I did," I say, angry at the injustice.

"And?"

"And she wrote you a reply. She must have lost it before giving it to you."

"A nice reply?"

"I expect so." My fingers are crossed behind my back.

"Well, then, you must have said something bad to her about me."

"I didn't, I swear."

He looks doubtful.

"It's true, Walter, honestly. I just put the note on her bed. I'm sure she doesn't even know who left it."

He stops kicking the path. His hat strays low over his eyes. His entire face is now wreathed in gloomy shade, unreadable. "What did she say when she got it? Something must have happened. She won't speak to me now."

"I really don't know," I lie, swallowing hard. "She doesn't confide in me."

He looks so crestfallen that I add, "I can't imagine anyone not liking you, Walter, even though you get so furious sometimes — but she must also be terribly tired with all this heat, so you'll just have to wait."

Pushing his cap back, he smiles crookedly. "I suppose so. I'm sorry I got annoyed with you, little Mouse."

"That's all right," I say. But it isn't. A large tear drips down my cheek and into my mouth. I taste salt, am reminded of the eggs in brine we used to eat at Passover. "You've made me cry." I almost spit out the words, surprising myself with my boldness. "I did nothing wrong, but you upset me anyway."

"Well, then, I apologize also for upsetting you, Esther," he says with exaggerated courtesy. "I didn't know you were that sensitive." I can hear in the long silence the song of a frog somewhere. Walter has just called me Esther. He never does that. My name sounds cold and hard and brassy, like a dirty coin, and I feel lonelier than ever.

"I hate it when you call me Esther. And I'm busy," I say, going inside.

Chapter Eight

This has been the most frightening day since we arrived. The man in the stinking coat, the one who's touched in the head and screams abuse at us every time we set foot on the path to the village, comes running into the barn and beats his arms and head against a wall. The sound is terrifying. I'm afraid his forehead will break like an eggshell and steaming brains will tumble out. Rose shoos him away with a broom. Shaking his fist at her, he yells something obscene before disappearing down the hill.

"I'm really tired of this," she says, as though he bursts in every day.

It isn't long before Inge, too, comes running. She's been down in the village leaving her watch to be fixed. She smells sweaty, and her short-cropped hair is spiky. "Listen," she cries. "France has surrendered to Germany."

"What?" Rose's voice cuts through the room, sharp as a meat cleaver.

"How can it be?" asks Naomi. "It can't be true, can it? Inge must be joking."

But Inge isn't. Not satisfied with Belgium, the Nazis have come looking for more land, more glory, and to threaten our safety. It's as if they follow us from place to place, black and forbidding. Suddenly the barn, dilapidated, inadequate, miserable, is our haven. I can't imagine leaving it.

Our directrice gathers together all the older children, and the boys' directeur, a meek little man with a stringy gray mustache, stands next to her as if to lend support. I'm shivering, gooseflesh breaking out along my arms and thighs. Walter is on the other side of the room. He seems almost unconcerned, busy with pencil and paper.

The directrice wrings her hands before placing them at her sides. Taking a loud, deep breath, she begins to speak. "You've probably been hearing rumors, so I want to clarify things for you. France *has* capitulated to Germany, but our part of France, the south, is still under French rule, so we needn't be worried, at least for the moment."

"Pah! That French government is just a front for the Nazis," Rose mutters with a grimace. "Call it French rule if you like, but it's really Nazi rule. If it was real French rule it would be finished." Her sleeves rolled up above her red elbows, her hair flying in all directions, she looks wild, angry, ready to do battle; but there's no one to do battle with. The directrice glares at her, and Rose runs back to the kitchen. We hear her pounding something, perhaps a turnip, against the table.

"Rose is upset," the directeur says gently. "She's upset so she doesn't know what she's saying."

"We're safe then?" asks Heinz, his freckles startling against the pale skin of his nose.

The directeur blinks several times and stares at the directrice for guidance.

"Well, I'm pretty sure we are," she says with nervous

conviction. "But if it looks like we aren't, we'll take action, so you needn't be alarmed."

"*Gott im Himmel.*" This, of course, is from my friend.

Eva sobs loudly, and immediately three boys, one of them Walter, rush over to her. Her hair may be cropped, her arms bony, but she's still pretty in a porcelain way. She reminds me of my Kammer & Reinhart baby doll from when I was little, her eyelashes long and dark, her mouth slightly open, her blue eyes bigger than ever as her face grows leaner. Her frailty, no doubt, makes her even more appealing to Walter. For the first time I can't find it in me to be jealous or irritated. I'm too weary. I'd like to spit, the way men do in the village, or scream with frustration, but I don't have the energy.

When the Nazis took over Belgium, we had to escape, and fast. What will happen now? We've already been pushed to the edge of the continent. There seems nowhere to go except into the woods or the water. I feel beaten down by hunger and filth and oppression. I can't stand the thought of another move.

The room is too quiet after the directrice leaves, a hollow sadness. My head itches, and I can almost hear, through the open window, the wild red poppies bowing to the breeze, rustling like tissue paper. How strange — even when war comes, even when people are at terrible risk, nature remains unchanged and uncaring. I can't rouse myself to go over to look at the crimson splash of the poppies daubing the fields. Every red splatter would be a shock, like spilt blood. I think instead of the lemon and almond trees at the botanical gardens in Berlin, the wild flowers in a forest near the city. I'm sure they'll bloom summer after summer, startling and lush. Disgusting. Their beauty is somehow grotesque, inappropriate, when people are suffering and dying. What has happened to my family? What will happen to me? These questions have become empty echoes.

I'd cry, like Eva, but with Walter gone to her, who will console me? I sniff instead. No one offers me a handkerchief or piece of rag. Still, no one is mean to me either.

As the afternoon flows into dusk and evening, voices stay low; the usual wretched fights over food and space and possessions, over who is friends with whom, are forgotten. Our fear, at least for this teardrop of a moment, has made us kind.

With a sharp jolt I realize that all the others are alone, too. We are like Noah's Ark, cut off from everything we love and understand, sailing along unsure of what we might find at the end of our journey. If there will be an end. It feels as though this will go on forever. I put my arm around Katerina, one of the younger children. She has blue sores all over her chest and legs. She whimpers, but to my surprise she doesn't pull away. Her small roundness reminds me of my little brother, Josef, and I take comfort and strength from that. We need to be brave.

Chapter Nine

Inge's watch has been fixed. She asks Rose if she can go and fetch it.

"Take someone with you," Rose advises, looking at me. "The streets are full of French soldiers waiting to be demobbed."

I don't want to go. "Look at my hair," I cry, running my hands through the harsh, dark stubble. "It's like toothbrush bristles."

"What does it matter?" Inge isn't even looking in my direction. "They're all strangers. They don't care."

I make a face.

"Bung a scarf over your head, then. Here, I'll lend you one — a scarf, not a head." She pulls out a kerchief from a messy pile of clothes and hands it to me, grinning. Then she waltzes out the door.

I follow reluctantly, feeling resentful.

A few steps and I want to turn back. There used to be only old people in the village and Pierre, the crazy man who screamed at us. Now there are soldiers everywhere, smoking, spitting, swearing. The war is over for them before it has really begun, and they've no one to turn their aggression on. There is something transient about them, yet edgy and sinister, although a few have baby faces and many appear no older than our boys.

"They'll be gone in a few days, most of them." Inge draws closer to me.

She retrieves her watch from the wizened man in the poky basement shop, and we climb the three stone steps to street level. Four or five soldiers, who did nothing but whistle at our backs on our way down, now close in, talking back and forth in rapid French, laughing, rolling their eyes.

Inge laughs back, but uncertainly. She's never uncertain, so I'm terrified. I stop dead and stare at the ground. The soldiers mill around us. No man has ever taken an interest in me before, not that way, but now that it's happening it's horrible.

Someone grabs my hand and pulls me away from Inge. His fingers press into my slippery palm. Someone else lunges at my breast through my flimsy dress, a flowered cotton that's much too small. "She's got big ones," he sniggers. "Wouldn't throw this Yid out of my bed." I smack him hard but he doesn't retreat.

"Your bad luck," says someone else. "You know what they say about Jew girls. They never give up the prize."

As if from far off, I hear Inge's voice. "Leave us alone. We're all on the same side. Get your hands off me, you idiots."

"I like a girl with a bit of fight in her," jeers one of the men.

It's a very hot day but I'm freezing. My body feels enormous, bigger than a mountain. Muscleless, boneless, unable to move. Their hands are all over me, squeezing, pinching. My mouth fills with bile.

Suddenly Pierre, the crazy man, swoops in, screaming, swearing, scattering our tormentors. He smells of dustbins and urinals and year-old sweat. But as he yells himself hoarse about evil Jews and dirty soldiers and the righteousness of the Lord, Inge grabs my arm and runs, dragging me behind her. The old people of the village look on placidly. A brindle dog pees against a tree. But all I can think of is my stupid worn-out dress and the way it pulls across my breasts. I'm afraid I'll come apart before Inge gets me home.

Night falls, hot and humid. We shutter the windows and push our beds, stools, and anything else we can find against the doors. Then we lie down in the tropical dark, waiting. My eyes stare into nothing, my pulse beats jaggedly in my throat.

At least we are all together now, boys and girls. The usual bedtime rules have been relaxed. Inge is curled on the floor. I lie near her. Walter, who's been almost unbearably sympathetic all afternoon, is sitting next to me holding my hand, and little Katerina has crept into my arms. Though I've scrubbed my body white where the soldiers grabbed me, I'm sure I'll never feel clean again, never feel safe. Even the touch of a friend, which I've always craved, is almost a torture. We are so squashed I can scarcely move.

It is very, very quiet except for the warm song of crickets and the occasional hoot of an owl. But we aren't fooled. The soldiers will come. A villager crept up to warn us at dusk.

Finally. The sound of men's voices, far off in the distance, hard to distinguish from the night insects. Perhaps it's only my imagination, inventing what I dread to hear. But now I can detect their boots on the gravel, and their lewd army songs littered with words I don't understand. There is a banging on the door, a shoving against the windows.

"Let us in, Yids," hoarse voices yell.

"Or send out the girls."

I can hardly breathe. My fingernails dig into the back of Walter's hand. His dig into mine, reminding me of the soldier in the village. This is Walter, I tell myself sternly, so I don't pull away. He is as scared as I am, I realize, has slid down, his free arm now slung across Katerina and me. He is shivering slightly, and I can feel his quick, shallow breath, his tawny hair against my cheek and eyelashes. Don't be afraid, I want to say. We'll be all right. But my voice won't come.

A shutter splinters, flooding the room with broken strips of moonbeam. For a second I see the directeur cowering, his eyes glazed with fear, his mustache an inky stain against his lip. Then Rose rushes to the window and sticks her arms through the hole in the shutter, blocking the light. What can she be doing? Whatever it is, it works. There is a scream and a moment's lull.

"Over here," she yells to us. "Pile up everything you can."

We are running in the dark, bumping into one another,

grabbing beds and stools from around the door, clothing from the floor, and pushing everything against the window. The soldiers are yodeling their filthy songs, shouting and laughing. The littlest children are screaming, Rose is yelling orders, Walter is mumbling numbers and I'm praying: *Hear, O Israel, the Lord our God, the Lord is one.*

God's not listening, I think, as the singing outside grows more insistent. But why should he listen now? He's clearly been asleep for years or we wouldn't be here in the first place. Katerina is sobbing loudly in my ear, and it galvanizes me into action. I rush too fast toward the window with a stool, slam my head hard against something sharp, most likely a piece of broken shutter. My forehead bangs on bits of furniture before I hit the floor, and I feel the teeth-clamping pain through my faint. It is midnight black, and I feel Yossi's eyes on me again. I slide back to him, to Mama and Papa. They stretch out their arms to me.

Much later, I awake. My head hurts horribly, but I'm in my own bed, in its usual place. Rose is bending over me, her back to the open door, and from either side of her, bright light, summer daylight, which makes her look like a dark, gruff angel, streams into my eyes.

"It's over, then?" My voice is a croak.

"You'll have a scar along your eyebrow for life," grumbles my nurse. "You really fell hard — and there's a lot of you to fall. Don't look so afraid. We scared them off. They're no better than Nazis, but most of them are gone today, back to their homes. Lucky those bastards were drunk." She puts a cool rag on my forehead, clucks her tongue, and goes outside.

A minute later she's back. "And by the way, Madame Directrice thinks there's no point in moving again — and nowhere to move to. So we're staying here, in this God-forsaken hole."

"Well, I *suppose* that's good news," I say, before falling asleep again.

Chapter Ten

The past keeps my mind occupied while I'm stuck in bed. Like Walter with his numbers, I examine what has happened, looking for order, clues. Sometimes I drift off, but more often I go back and forth over things, trying to make sense of them.

Even before Yossi was beaten up, we knew we had problems. Nazi slogans were scrawled everywhere. And every day our headmistress would click her heels, shout "*Heil* Hitler" and raise the flag with its disgusting swastika as she glared at the few of us Jewish children still in the school. But Yossi was my first taste of violence. I screamed at his attacker — I couldn't help myself. Then, alarmed at my own stupidity, I scrambled back through the window and vomited into the washbasin on the bureau. I hated everything about Hitler, everything about the stinking Nazis, and I knew I must get away before they came after me, too.

Two days later, after getting advice from the Jewish Agency, I wrote to register with the Cultural Society in Belgium, asking if they could help me leave Germany. Mama watched me disapprovingly as I penned and blotted the letter, licked the envelope. She banged her wooden spoon on the kitchen table till flour flew up in a cloud, and cut out the knish dough for supper as if she were stabbing someone.

"You're still a child."

"Old enough to do what I need to."

"A child shouldn't answer back. And a child doesn't make decisions for herself."

"I told you. I'm not a child."

"We're a family." Her words were short and sharp. "And families stick together, no matter what. My parents kept us all together through the pogroms, the anti-Jewish hatred in Poland. We all survived. If we hadn't, you wouldn't be here now."

"But I am here. I'm alive and I want to stay that way."

"You will. Nothing will happen."

"Ha!"

"I only hope your children treat you the way you're treating me — then maybe you'll understand."

Her face was as sour as spring apples, but I managed to keep my mouth shut, slipping out of the apartment as soon as I could to mail my request.

After waiting for a reply for weeks, hanging around in a hopeful dream, I realized I wasn't going to receive one.

"Perhaps you're too young," suggested Mama, a lightness twining into the timbre of her voice. "But it's for the best, Esther-leh. We don't want to split up the family. Things will get better, you'll see."

But things didn't get better.

I was expelled from school after jumping out of one of the big gymnasium windows. I did it because the other girls were teasing me as usual, and, after trying to stay quiet and inconspicuous for weeks, I couldn't stand it any longer.

"Look at the fat Yid," said Annalotte, as I cleaned the blackboard. "Look how her dress rides up when she lifts her arms. You can see everything she's got."

"At least I've got *something,* Flat Chest."

"Egg-bread Esther," giggled someone else. "Fraülein Jew Cake 1938."

That was it. I ran straight to the window and took a giant leap, flattening the petunia bed by the flagpole. Catching sight of the girls inside, who were pointing and giggling, I shook my fist at them.

"Jews," the headmistress said bitterly to my teacher, after she'd pronounced my sentence. "What do you expect?"

"What could have got into your head?" Papa said, after he'd recovered from his shock.

"You have no idea, Papa, how horrid they all are to me."

"But now there's no book learning for you."

"I'd have had to leave anyway. New Nazi rule: no Jewish children allowed in German schools."

"No school? That's impossible. Every child needs an education."

"It's true, Mottel," Mama told him as she laid supper on the table. "I heard it myself this afternoon. What is the world coming to?"

Mama and Papa might be scandalized, but I didn't mind. Now I could stand by the kosher butcher's and watch with delight as the German children streamed by on their way to servitude. I feel light as air remembering those few delicious days.

But I couldn't spend my days playing in the park, much as I wanted to. Jewish children, apparently, were no longer allowed on the grass, either. A big sign said, "Jews and dogs not wanted here." Now I was a dog. I had nowhere safe to go. Instead I helped Mama, who was trying to keep everything just as it had always been, even though our savings were disappearing down a big hole.

Papa was a baker because his father had been a baker. "You'll be a baker, too," he admonished my little brother, wagging his finger at him. Josef just giggled, but being a baker was a good trade, because no matter how poor people were, they still needed bread. So why was business so bad lately? Papa would come upstairs exhausted after working since early morning, still smelling of yeast but with barely a coin to show for it.

"What's happening, Mottel?" protested Mama, her round face swollen into an uneven network of little mounds and creases. "You've always done so well — and now there's no money for a Sabbath chicken?" Sabbath meant everything to Mama. One pass of her hands above the candles as she recited the *Shabbos* prayers, one glance at our shining faces as we devoured her chicken soup with *knaidlech*, could set her up for the week. My mouth waters as I think of those puffy dumplings and fragrant broth now. I've eaten nothing good for the longest time.

"The gentiles aren't allowed to buy at our shops any more." Papa looked ashen. Often at night I could hear him wheezing, the air whistling in and out of his lungs in a dull, miserable tune. It frightened me. I put my pillow over my head so I didn't have to hear it.

"What's that to us? We sell Jewish bread. Gentiles don't want it. They eat that nasty black pumpernickel or poisonous white nothing bread."

"That's true," replied Papa. "But the Jews aren't buying either. Without gentile business they haven't got two pennies to rub together. I'm going to bed, Rifka, my dear. I'm going to wrap myself up and sweat off this cough. Only God knows how long I'll be able to keep the store going."

Fall arrived, harsh and gray. The apartment grew cold as ice after we used the last of the coal. Following a downpour of sleet, Mama made a big decision: "Fuel is more important than keeping up appearances."

During the next week she sold some of our furniture, gasping at the low price she was offered. First the bureau in the bedroom vanished, leaving a dirty yellow imprint on the wall. Then someone bought the plant stand in the living room. Our small apartment began to look shabbily empty as other pieces that Mama had polished diligently for years disappeared with the gentiles who tramped mud up and down the stairs as if they were at an auction. But at least we were warm.

Mama had never made important choices before. That had always been Papa's department. Now if she asked him to do anything, he'd reply, "I'm too ill, my dear — you decide," and disappear into the bedroom.

Suddenly she was dickering with buyers, speaking to our creditors, preparing the dough and setting it to rise at four in the morning. We weren't even the owners any more. A gentile had bought — or, rather, appropriated — the bakery and our apartment. We had to pay him rent. *The absentee landlord,* Mama called him. Absent except when the rent was due.

Her plumpness fell away till she was all lines and sharp angles. She nagged at little Josef and me and treated

Papa very strangely. One minute she was fretting over his illness: "Take care of yourself, Mottel," she would beg. "For my sake. For the children's, if not your own." The next she was complaining, "You're a good for nothing who can't even make a decent living. Oy yoy, what will become of us all?"

"How can you talk to Papa like that?" I demanded, but she didn't answer. I hated being in the apartment, hated Mama's bad humor and Papa's sickness, but outside was worse. Anti-Semitic messages were scrawled across the sidewalk, gangs of youths rampaged through the streets for amusement. Nazi pigs! I thought viciously. But I was — and still am — deeply troubled. I'm a Jew by accident of birth. Suppose I was born a gentile? Would I now be calling for the death of the Jews? Mama spoke badly of all gentiles. Papa, who, like Mama, had grown up in Poland, hated the Poles. Some of the girls here hate other girls, fight with the less popular boys, even though we're all Jewish. Do we human beings always need someone to hate? The thought shocks me, gnaws at me.

One night, when we were all asleep in the back bedroom, there was a loud rap on the apartment door. The Nazis had forced their way through the store and up the stairs. Bleary-eyed and shivering, we crept into the hall.

"Mottel Wilinski? We are arresting you and every Jewish man of Polish descent. You are a threat to the Fatherland."

"He's sick," screamed Mama. "You can't take him."

But in a moment poor Papa, bent and wheezing, had gone, and Mama was rushing after the truck they had thrown him into. She kicked and yelled, screamed at them to give him back as she chased them, with Josef in her arms, all the way to the main road. Her feet were bare, her nightdress flapping around her ankles. The truck took a sharp turn behind tall buildings and vanished, its tires screeching, as Mama stood in front of the now-boarded-up butcher's, one arm against the wall, the other holding my brother. She had lost her anger, was deflated as an empty flour sack. I was watching, petrified, from the roof. I sobbed then because I knew I would never see my papa again. I sobbed, too, because I knew they could take me, and I would die. I sob now, thinking about it.

Chapter Eleven

My dearest Mama,

I need to tell you that we've moved to a castle called Château la Blaize. Please, please, try to get a response to me. I can't stand the silence. I worry so much about you and little Josef. My mind fills with all sorts of horrible pictures of what might have happened to you both, and though I try to shake free of them, they return in nightmares when I have no defense. So I really need to hear from you, Mama.

At first, when we left Belgium, we stayed in a big barn in the grounds. The directeur and directrice (I've told you about them) went back to Belgium as soon as the authorities allowed them to. They weren't Jewish, they were Belgians, so they'll be safe enough. After they went, we got a horrid directeur, strict as anything, who made us say grace — not Jewish prayers — before eating and made us stand in lines for hours every day — well, it seemed like hours. He made us eat everything on our plates and scrape them clean with a spoon. I wouldn't complain — it's war and there's little enough to eat anyway, so we should be grateful for anything — but some of it was pig meat, traif, with the bristles still on. It made me throw up. Ugh.

The new directeur locked my friend Walter up for swearing in German — only French is allowed and no swearing either — and fed him bread and water for a week. I managed to sneak some of my rations in to him — poor Walter's thin as a rail and I can certainly spare it. Now don't you worry. I'm still huge, a grobbe moid. A tub of a thing. Or as you'd have it, your zaftige schaine maidel — your plump, pretty girl. Nothing seems to take the weight off me.

Anyhow, everybody hated the new directeur — we called him Monsieur Pig-Face behind his back — and in the end he left, creeping out in the middle of the night with everything of any value.

When we first arrived, the castle was occupied by one solitary man. It seemed very unfair. But then the police came and arrested him — and I felt guilty for having wished he'd disappear.

They told us he was a British sympathizer — and a Jew, of course.

The villagers know we're Jewish, but as the policeman said afterwards, "There are Jews and Jews. He was a bad one." As if the man were a rotten apple they'd found at the bottom of the barrel. Might I be a rotten apple? I couldn't sleep for days.

Sometimes I see the old owner about the place, although of course it's only my imagination. Rose told me the château's from the fifteenth century, so it's had plenty of owners and maybe there's a ghost. I wonder who's lived here, and how they left or died — or were removed. Will we be removed, too? And if we are, what will happen to us? Who will stay here after us? Gruesome thoughts. I'm sorry.

You shouldn't think my mind is taken up only with sadness. This place is beautiful, Mama, more beautiful than you can imagine. It's a proper castle, with tall, graceful towers and flowering plants and trees like at the botanical gardens. And so much space! It took us weeks to clean — some of the rooms hadn't even been opened for maybe hundreds of years — but it was worth it.

It's lovely outside, too. There are long paths through the hills. The mountains, the Pyrenees, are far off, but they hide the horizon and sometimes their tops vanish into the clouds. It's like a fairy-story castle. I try to walk every day when it's not too hot, as Rose says that physical activity is good for me. I do exercises, too. I'd so like to look willowy. I need to be strong.

There are only a few bad things. Some of the girls are still horrid. Werner ran away after they found out he'd stolen some raspberry jam that Rose had made from wild berries. He must have been awfully hungry — we all are, and the jam was supposed to be shared among all of us — but those girls badgered him till he couldn't stand it any longer. No one knows where he's gone, and I'm scared he might have been turned over to the Nazis.

But there's good news, too. Heinz, a tall red-haired boy — I think I've told you about him — has gone to America to be adopted by a cousin. I'm pleased for him but sad he's left, as he was never unkind to me. Walter is still here, though. I don't know what I'd do without him. He treats me like his little sister when he isn't too busy to remember me, which is almost all the time. Just kidding.

Well, that's all my news. Again, Mama, please, please write if you can. I miss you so much and need to know that you're well. It's bad enough not knowing what happened to Papa. But not knowing how you and Josef are doing — I can't stand that.

I'm afraid I was never a very good daughter. I didn't appreciate you enough. But I'll make up for it when this horrid war's over and we can all be together again, I promise.

Lots and lots and lots of love,

Esther

Chapter Twelve

"I'm incredibly interested in the Knights Templar," Walter is saying to Eva.

We're in the yard, supposedly studying. The two of them are sitting across from me, poring over Walter's book. How very close they are to each other — as he slides lower in his seat to speak in her ear, I feel a miserable scowl starting around the corners of my mouth and radiating up to my forehead. I try to smooth my brow, raise my hand as a screen, but can still see the lovebirds through my fingers. I can't believe she's playing up to him. She and her cronies tease me for doing the same thing.

"Who is smitten by the great Walter Stein, scourge of the Nazis?" she said one bedtime. "Who hangs on his every word? Could it be *little* Esther the *mouse*?" I wanted to die.

"I hear tell he thinks he can topple the Nazis with Kabbalah," grinned Lisel, combing her thin dark hair. It gleamed as blackly in the evening light as oil on water. "Maybe he'll throw a few spells Esther's way, just for practice. Might be hard to knock *her* over though."

"Not if the way she looks at him is any indication," giggled Eva, her harsh words sending me scrambling under the covers. "Shut up, shut up," I muttered into the darkness, furious, but no one could hear me.

"I think the Knights might be the answer to my problem," Walter is saying now. His hand is on Eva's knee. She doesn't remove it. "Do you know who they were?"

"No," she replies, her small tinkling laugh irritating me beyond reason.

"They were the knowledge keepers in the Holy Land during the Crusades. They guarded the Temple Mount and had clandestine books and understood magic. They might have known where the Holy Grail was hidden ... Perhaps their knowledge will help me defeat Hitler."

I can see Eva doesn't know what "clandestine" means. She squirms. "Such a topic for a Jewish boy."

"We have to examine everything if we're going to beat this monster." Walter looks very stern. He just needs glasses to be the perfect professor. "I think the Freemasons know the secrets of the Knights Templar ... the Great Arcanum ... that's why the Vichy government is so down on them."

"The great what?"

"Arcanum, Eva — the huge secret of the workings of the universe. Do you have any idea how pretty you look when you bite your lip that way?"

With the merest hint of a sneer, which Walter doesn't see, Eva gets up and walks away. Soon she's giggling with her friends across the courtyard. Walter flushes crimson and goes back to his book.

I sidle over to him. "Aren't you interested in gematria any more, Walter?"

"Of course I am. I'm just adding more strings to my bow, that's all. Were you listening to us, Mouse?" He narrows his eyes in his usual suspicious way. Some days he seems to think that the whole world is against him.

"No, but I couldn't help hearing. You didn't exactly keep your voices down." I take a deep breath, courage for what I'm about to say. "She's not worth it, you know."

"Not worth what?" His eyes are dangerous, with just a glimmer of yellow. His back is rigid.

"She ... she's not worth all the attention you shower on her. *I'm* interested in what you have to say," I complain. "But you never tell me anything."

He relaxes. One bony foot shoots out suddenly. "Sure I do. But it makes you nervous and you don't really understand. Anyhow, if you really want to know, I'm not that keen on Eva any more, even though she's the prettiest girl I've ever seen. But I sometimes have the feeling — wrong, I'm sure — that she's laughing at me behind my back."

"I'm sure you *are* wrong — about the laughing, I mean." I'm ecstatic, but want to change the subject fast before he talks himself back into liking her or, worse, before I do it for him. "I hate to tell you this, big brother, but you forgot my birthday. I'm sixteen today."

Walter isn't listening. "Inge, on the other hand," he says, folding his hands behind his head and gazing dreamily at the mountains, "Inge is a girl to be reckoned with. Tall, intelligent, good-humored, attractive in an almost masculine way. Nothing fazes her. There's a strength to her I wouldn't mind having myself. And she'd know what 'arcanum' means."

"For sure." I'm entirely disgusted.

"Mademoiselle Inspiration. That's my name for her."
He's still a little flushed.

"How appropriate." Pulling on wisps of my stubby hair
till I want to cry out in pain, I can't look at him. "What is
it exactly she inspires, Walter?" I say sarcastically, a short
curl still wound around my forefinger.

He ignores me. "Yep, she's better than Eva the ice
maiden any day."

My head comes up, my voice shrill. "Do you have to
be in love all the time?"

"Who said I was in love? And what's it to you? *Mein
Gott,* why are you always bothering me?"

"Bothering you? *You're* the one bothering *me* with
your stupid talk." But my eyes spike with sudden tears.

Walter hates when I cry. He snaps his book shut and
strides inside.

Two minutes later he is back, his face contorted into
a lopsided grin. "Your head looks much better. Mouse hair
growing back."

"Humph." I know he's trying to pacify me. It won't work.

"Did you say it was your birthday, Mouse?"

I don't answer, still feel annoyed and bruised. But my
silence is never a problem for Walter.

"Sixteen, eh? Many happy returns. Here, this is for
you. My mother, God bless and keep her, gave it to me
when I left Germany." He holds out a thin gold chain with
a Star of David on it and drops it in my lap, where it blazes
softly, like a spiraling dazzle of sun on water. I stare at the
necklace, stunned with wonder. We both believe, know

with a clammy certainty, that Walter's mother and the rest of his family are dead. Yet he has passed on her gift, her *Mogen David*, to me.

We forget that we live a magical existence — we are schooled and disciplined like regular children living a regular life, we're protected. Though we're often scared, this château is an oasis in a desert of destruction.

"Little sister Mouse," he whispers, "you are my family now."

Overwhelmed by his generosity, by his acceptance of me as kindred, I can't trust myself to speak. I give him a quick, embarrassed hug. He hugs me back. Still grinning, he shrugs and strolls away.

Chapter Thirteen

Why is he so dear to me? When did he first speak to me?
First realize I existed?

It was in the classroom in Belgium. His face, what I
could see of it, was in shadow. He was sitting in front of
me and slightly to my right, his head propped by his fist,
his elbow on the desk. A big window bathed the room in
milky light. I couldn't take my eyes off him, though his
lids were all but closed and his profile angular, forbidding.

"Mademoiselle, are you listening? How many times do
I have to repeat the same things over and over?" The
boys' directeur, middle-aged and black-suited, was staring
at me with profound irritation. Naomi giggled. A chair
scraped, a paper dart bounced across my desk.

"I'm sorry, monsieur. I didn't quite hear what it was
you asked."

"*Mein Gott,*" groaned Walter, but too softly to be heard
by our teacher. His legs, far too long to remain imprisoned
by the desk, shot out from under it.

"I asked, mademoiselle — and you would have heard
had you been listening, had you not been far more
interested in those around you — that you translate from
the German: 'There are mice in the barn. They are eating
the grain.'"

What did we have to know that for? The war was coming. How useful would it be to talk about mice? "Um, il y'a de souris dans le ... le ... le ..." I stuttered hopelessly, before lapsing into miserable and shamed silence.

"God save me from dogs and children," muttered Walter. I couldn't see him through my sudden blur of tears, didn't have to. I began to cry, loud embarrassing sobs. Eva and Greta exchanged smirks, rolled their eyes.

"Ah, the Jewish peasant," grinned Eva. "She just doesn't know how to behave."

"Shut up," I hissed, mostly to her because I didn't dare say anything to Walter. My chair tipped back, slamming against the floor, and I rushed from the room.

Two days later, as I slipped into class, trying to be unobtrusive, Walter stopped me. He'd been lolling against the wall as I tried to inch past him. I hadn't realized — why would I? — that he was waiting for me.

"Mouse?" he said tentatively, pushing away from the wall. He could have been talking to anyone. But he was staring into my eyes.

"Please let me by." My pulse throbbed in my throat. I didn't need any more of his contempt.

"I'm sorry, but I don't know your name, and you are like a little mouse — easily startled — with that light-brown hair falling around your face. A little field mouse. Besides, all that trouble was over a mouse ... une petite souris."

I could feel the blush rising to my forehead. No one ever called me "little." "My name's Esther ..."

"Esther, then." His voice, when untinged by anger, was like apples and honey. I think I was half in love with him already.

"But you can call me Mouse if you want to. I quite like it." It was a lot better than what some other people were calling me, but I didn't have the courage to say so. We were both speaking German, and had to lean in so we wouldn't be discovered. His tawny hair had fallen forward across his forehead and over one eye so he looked a little like a pirate. It felt almost intimate, our conversation, though I now realize there was very little intimate about it.

"I'm sorry. I was being unkind to you ... about you. It didn't occur to me that you'd hear. I shouldn't have done it anyway — I just get very impatient. It's all so stupid and so slow. What are we doing in there when there's a war brewing?"

"You don't need to apologize."

"I apologize all the time. When you've got a mouth as big as the Dead Sea, you have to if you want to survive." He smiled, a curious smile, lazy but warm, that lit his amber eyes. The almost concave line of his cheek softened. He took my hand.

"Well, thank you," I murmured, shy. I wouldn't have stepped away for the world, but at that moment the teacher called us to order, and I scuttled to my desk.

Chapter Fourteen

When what milk we can get sours so fast it has to be kept in the cellar, when the day is so hot the air in the castle steams like a Turkish bath, we spend most of our free time outside. Walter, despite his admiration of Inge, has inexplicably gone back to his pursuit of Eva. Perhaps she smiled at him again.

One day, while taking my habitual walk up the mountain, I come across the two of them in the woods. They're both clearly upset and so caught up in an argument they don't notice me. I duck behind a huge tree, unable to stop myself listening to her angry charges, his agitated responses. I shouldn't be here. It's spying. But I can't get my feet to move. Besides, they're talking about me.

"Esther, the idiot mouse — she's your favorite — you're always hanging around in corners whispering with her."

"*Gott im Himmel,* that's the silliest nonsense I ever heard."

"No, it's not, it's true. You know it is. You care for her more than anyone, so why are you always traipsing after me?"

"Eva …" His tone, sharp and pleading, has entirely lost its apple-honey flavor.

"Yesterday you even had your arm around her, and you gave her your *Mogen David* a while ago. I've seen it around her stupid, fat neck."

I almost faint, want to die, but at least Walter will defend me. I'm certain of it.

"Listen, Eva, Esther Wilinski means nothing to me. She's just a kid I feel sorry for, that's all."

Traitor. I could easily kill him.

"Right," Eva sneers.

I can see by the angular thrust of his head, the compression of his lips, that Walter's desire to please is giving way to his quick, cold rage, and I hope, in spite of my anger at him, that he'll rip her apart, horrible pig that she is. "I'm sorry. I won't ever mention the subject again. I should have known better than to tell you how I felt," he spits, spinning away from her.

"Well." Eva goes after him, touches his arm. "If you're sure you don't care for her ... well then, I believe you." Gloat coats her voice. I wince.

"Of course I'm sure. Absolutely." A moment's silence, broken by the sharp cry of a bird, maybe a crow, somewhere above. "I just need ... a bit more from you — if you like me, too."

"More?" She looks startled. "I've no idea what you mean."

"Well, it's like when I sent that note to you. You never answered it."

"Of course I answered it," says Eva. "I gave my reply to your peasant friend to deliver."

The forest is suddenly a nightmare. I need to get away.

But as I take a first tentative step, a twig snaps like a bone cracking. Walter stares right at me. I stand transfixed, as if the two of us are alone on the mountain. His face contorts with the pain of betrayal. I can't bear to dwell on how I tore up the stupid note or how much he's hurt me since. I crash away through the bushes. A low branch slashes my cheek, but I don't care. I hate everyone and everything.

After that day, Walter Stein stops calling me Mouse, stops calling me his little sister, stops talking to me altogether. It's as if I'm invisible. I suppose he's angry with me, or ashamed, or maybe afraid that Eva might work out that I mean something to him after all — if I still do. Everything is hopeless.

One morning, after at least three weeks of his silence and my misery, I catch sight of him in the hall talking to a couple of the girls. I tear the *Mogen David* off my neck in a hot fury, breaking the chain, and throw both at his feet. I'm amazed to discover I have been carrying around so much anger. He bends down slowly, almost sorrowfully, to pick them up. I want to kick him. The knobs of his skinny back are visible through the thin fabric of his shirt. The star, slipping off the chain, bounces and rolls, to rest close to my shoe. I boot it away hard and it arcs across the room, disappearing under a bookshelf. There are others in the hall — someone has been whispering about listening to a contraband radio and the lies of the Vichy government — and everyone comes to a dead halt. I hear one low, throaty giggle, which I'm almost sure is Eva. Perhaps she has the grace to feel embarrassed. More likely she's enjoying my wretchedness.

Retrieving the star, Walter stuffs it into his pocket. His yellow irises are catlike, washed with tears. He looks pathetic, and immediately I feel sorry for him. I rush away, my fingers clutching my stupid fat neck.

After that, even when he realizes he doesn't stand a chance with Eva, even when I'm sure he understands she's been leading him on in the most disgusting way, we just glare at each other. I can't relax the muscles in my face or I might cry in front of him; my eyes feel so huge I think they may explode out of my head. In the end, I learn not to look at him. I am more broken than the *Mogen David,* but something in me is too proud, I suppose: I can never bring myself to apologize. And neither, apparently, can he.

Chapter Fifteen

Horrid spoiled girls — ridiculous and mean. They hate me because I'm fat. Because I'm Old Jewish. Because I'm a baker's daughter, and their fathers were all doctors and dentists and professors, or so they claim. Greta even refused to pass me the bread at breakfast, saying I don't need as much food as the rest of them. And horrid, treacherous Walter, with his horrid crushes. Even he can't see through to the real me. If there is a real me.

Why did I ever even think of leaving Germany? I have to get out of here. I'll make my way back to Mama, back to the bakery in Berlin. I want to be safe, loved, looked after. She was right, I should have listened to her.

The lights are out. It's about ten o'clock, and a sullen moon gleams along the walls. Slowly, quietly, I feel for my clothes and coat. Even though it's still summer, I wear as much as I can because what's not on me will be left behind. I drag on my boots, tiptoe to the large window in the hall. Wresting it half open, which is all I can manage, I climb onto the sill, crouching to avoid the sash. It's a whole, steep story down to the yard, but there's little chance of creeping down the stairs and out the door without being caught. Rose is acting directrice till the Red Cross can find someone else brainless enough to take on the job. She prowls around for hours after lights out. She's never had this kind of responsibility before and is trying to make sure nothing bad happens to us. No wonder she's exhausted mornings.

I imagine myself floating, flying like an angel, drifting to earth with a soft bump. Then I'll find my way home. That's how I am when it comes to windows. My anger or frustration gets me there, poised to jump, and then nothing can make me change my mind. I know I'm being stupid, but I can't seem to stop myself. Blind obstinacy, Mama would say. Tut, tut.

"Well, here goes," I whisper, arrowing my arms like a diver. I push off, waiting to feel outside air against my cheeks like water rushing past. Instead I'm grabbed from behind, pulled violently. I crash backwards into the hall, landing hard on someone. I swing around in a fury. Inge's lying flat on her back, gasping. It's not surprising. I'd knock the wind out of anybody.

"What in hell do you think you're doing?" she pants.

"None of your business. Getting away from here, if you must know."

"Lucky I was awake. The fall would probably kill you, you idiot. Come back to bed before Rose shows up."

She marshals me back into the dormitory and sees me safely tucked up before muttering into the dark, "I know the other girls are mean to you, that Walter has let you down, and I'm sorry for that. I think we must be on edge because we know something even more awful is going to happen. But Esther, there's a war on. This is a safe place. It's much worse out there. You'd never get home — if home still exists."

Inge's eyes glitter in the dark. She speaks with a fierceness I didn't know she possessed. Her intensity leaves me feeling even more wretched, more alone, although she's trying to console me.

"I'm all right now," I whisper. "Thanks. Go to bed."

She slips into her bed, next to mine. When I'm absolutely sure she's asleep, I dress for the second time, my fingers, numbed by exhaustion, working clumsily at my cardigan buttons. Creeping back into the hall, I clamber onto the sill and launch myself out of the window, soaring into the past, going home.

Instead, I break my stupid wrist.

"You're lucky it wasn't your neck," clucks Rose. For a week, everyone stares at me in disbelief, giggles at my huge bandage. Now I even have a fat hand. Walter looks the other way, pained. Even Inge is annoyed. I've made a complete fool of myself. What was I so set on getting back to anyway?

Chapter Sixteen

I felt glee, mixed with terror and guilt, when a letter finally arrived from the Cultural Society. I was to go to the train station the following Wednesday. From there I would be sent to Belgium. *This will save me,* I thought. *This will keep me alive.* Immediately I felt like a traitor. How could I leave Mama and Josef?

"You don't have to go," sobbed Mama, still distraught over Papa's disappearance. "It's only men the Nazis want to get rid of. Stay safe here with Josef and me."

But Jews were scrambling to get out of Germany any way they could, and our street was half-deserted. Those left looked lost and hopeless. I was terrified of leaving, but I couldn't stay, even though I wasn't sure I had the right to decide. "No, I'm going," I replied. "There's no safety here anymore."

Mama made everything so hard. She begged and cried. "How can I manage home and store without your help? Without Papa there's no one but you and me to carry on. And what will become of your brother? I can't look after the store and him."

"Mama," I replied as kindly as I could, "you must apply for a visa. We've talked about this over and over. I'll meet you in Belgium. We'll all be safe. I have to go. I'm afraid I'll die if I stay here. I'm afraid you'll die, too. Can't you understand?"

I couldn't bear to look at her tear-streaked face, her runny nose. I wanted to tell her she was putting too much responsibility on me, burdening me with her grown-up worries, but I didn't dare. Traitorously, I packed my clothes in a suitcase, folding them carefully, slowly, neatly, as though calm could remake the situation, undo the hurt I was causing. She watched me silently, too exhausted to fight, the hollows around her eyes frightening, skull-like. Later, she would fight. Sometimes our battles went on all night.

"How can you leave me?" she'd yell. "What would your papa say?"

"He'd say, 'Get out while you can.'"

"You're a miserable, thankless child."

"And you're a heartless mother." I'd turn my back on her, try to read, sing, anything to drown her out. I cringe now at my cruelty.

"Look at me when I'm talking to you. And stop that racket. I only want what's best for you. You're just too selfish to see it."

"No, Mama. You're the selfish one. You want to keep me here even if it kills me."

"I only want to protect you. Why can't you see that?"

"Because it's not true." And then I said the awful words — "I hate you" — cold as icicles. I'd never said them before, and I don't know where they came from. They weren't true, but after that there was silence.

A week later, still feeling like a traitor, still battered by argument, I was on the train to Brussels, in a compartment with a dozen other Jewish girls, all daintier and prettier than I. Behind me at the station was Mama, carrying my little brother. She stood waving, half obscured by the hissing steam that billowed from the engine. I'd taken a mind picture of their downcast faces, committing them to memory in case I shouldn't see them again for a long time. "Mama," I whisper now in the dark, "why didn't you come?" But she can't hear me. I can't even conjure up the comfortable mother smell of her anymore.

Rose calls me into her office two days later, asks me to sit, and sets a cup of herb tea next to me as I nurse my bad arm. Never one to mince words, she immediately tells me she's received a message from a contact in Berlin. My mother and brother have been deported to Poland. "Sent East" is what Rose says, but I know only too well what that means. Jews who are sent east disappear and no one ever hears from them again.

At first, I can't take in the news, and I ask her to repeat it. She does, twice, each telling a little more embroidered by her and real to me. Inconsolable, I curl up in a high corner of one of the château towers and sob. My one photograph of my family, taken on a summer outing at the zoo, is locked in my fist. My brother stares at the camera, little and unsmiling, with ice cream dribbling down his chin. Mama is dabbing it off with a bit of spit on the corner of a hankie while Papa looks on. I'm in the picture, too, eyes shut, grinning. My aunt must have taken it before we were all posed properly. Has she been sent east, too?

How could we not have known what lay in store for us? How could we not have stood together and seen the past and the future merge like two great rivers? Then perhaps we'd all be together now in England or America. I can't, I mustn't think like this. And perhaps I should try not to think of them, either. It keeps them alive for me, but it's too painful, and useless.

After a while, I peer out the small, arched window of the tower. Walter is in the yard, his nose buried in a book, several scraps of paper lying beneath his chair. One escapes, flies off on the hot southerly breeze. He gazes after it with a bemused expression but makes no effort to fetch it.

Now Walter is all the family I have. I can't bear for anything to happen to him. Oblivious to my thoughts, he walks inside, and I suddenly remember: Walter's still not speaking to me. He barely seems to know I exist.

Chapter Seventeen

We have a new directrice, Madame Mallon, but behind her back everyone calls her Madame Malheur — or sometimes even Hitler. For a change we're united — united in our hatred of Madame Misfortune, though our unity doesn't last long. She's tall and unbending, with a single eyebrow straight across her forehead. Like Monsieur Pig-Face, she argues with Rose and runs Château la Blaize like an army camp. A tight ship, she calls it. I think her father was a sea captain. He probably made sailors walk the plank. Suddenly we have to make our beds with hospital corners, sweep and dust before breakfast, say grace before meals. She is so like Pig-Face, it's uncanny. Perhaps there's a special Red Cross training college for directeurs, where they teach people how to be rigidly cold. Maybe she came here for the money. Rose says that being a directrice pays well, steady employment in bad times. She says it attracts the worst people. But perhaps that's sour grapes because she didn't get the job.

School has become regimented, even for the older students, and we aren't allowed to speak in class or even at meals without permission. All afternoon there are chores for the older girls, and we also learn shorthand and typing — sharing our two decrepit typewriters. The boys work for the local farmers. Madame Malheur believes that idleness spawns wickedness. There is wickedness anyway. Some of the older students have a radio stolen from the village — strictly forbidden because Madame believes reports of the war can only upset us. They use it less to find out what's going on than to exclude the rest of us. They listen to the BBC and Radio Vichy, but never pass anything on except the occasional false story. Knowing what's happening is a valuable weapon, even here.

"Don't tell the others what the Allies are doing," Naomi warns Karl as he heads out for the fields. She is flaunting it, dangling information in front of those of us still ignorant of world events.

"I won't. I have too much to do to think about that anyhow."

"What *are* the Allies doing?" asks Walter innocently. He is wearing a torn shirt and shabby shorts, with an old tweed jacket over top. His knobby knees look like the foothills of the Pyrenees.

"Wouldn't you like to know," Eva smirks and winks at Lisel. I want to punch her.

"It's so unfair," complains Greta, watching the boys leave. "I'd rather be planting crops than this." Her hands are red and scabby from washing pots. I don't care what I do — any enforced routine is a relief. It lines up the present so I don't think too often about the past or the future. I don't even care that I can't listen to the radio. What can the broadcasts bring except the bad news we already get through the grapevine? Besides, who can listen to both the Allied and Vichy broadcasts and sift the truth from the propaganda?

Walter doesn't get to hear anything, either, so I feel he

should be kinder to me. But he's not. He stares right through me, his eyes like polished stones. In my quiet moments — at bedtime or early in the morning — I punish myself for his silence. Everything is entirely my fault. I feel his presence everywhere, but never approach him or meet his baleful amber glare. Instead, whenever I catch sight of him, I find Inge or Katerina and laugh too loudly, talk too much, flap my arms around in broad, uncharacteristic gestures. Afterward, I feel really stupid. And Walter moves about like a wraith, desperately unhappy, it seems. But that might be wishful thinking.

"Always there is nowhere without you," I scrawl on a scrap of paper, hardly understanding the words and never daring to pass him the message. Instead, I scrunch it up and toss it in the garbage. I pass by the bin several times that day, itching to take it back out, and in the evening I do, sliding it under my pillow and crying quietly into my blanket when everybody else is asleep. It is the last frail link between Walter and me.

The next morning I throw it away for good.

I faint in the afternoon from lack of food. Everything sticks in my throat because Walter is still ignoring me, and I can barely swallow a mouthful. But I'm sure I've not lost any weight. I am meant to be big and lumpy. My backside's massive. I remind me of my mother, feel a hot flush of guilt for the thought.

Eva pretends to be helpful. "You look all right coming," she says almost sympathetically, "but don't turn your back on anyone."

"I have big bones," I mutter. "It's not my fault."

"Since when are there bones in your ass?"

"Well, who are you to talk? Don't turn sideways — you'll disappear." But nothing I can say hurts her. Laughing merrily, she goes over to the other side of the dormitory and huddles with Greta and Lisel. I hear muffled sounds. They are listening to the radio, hidden beneath a pillow.

Inge comes and sits by me. She's decided she wants to put on a play to cheer everyone up.

"A play? Nothing classical, I hope." I hardly see myself as Juliet.

"I thought we could make something up." She grins. "Get all the big guys involved, Naomi, Lisel, Manfred ..."

"Don't say Walter," I implore.

"Walter, too. He's great at conspiracies. He'll think up the best adventure — Knights Templar, King Arthur and the Holy Grail, the Merovingian kings, or something equally spectacular. You have to stop being angry at him, Ess. Act normal, don't get too loud or too soft all of a sudden when you catch sight of him. Speak to him nonchalantly, like you do with the other boys."

"Nonchalantly, ha. I barely speak to the other boys at all. Besides, I never want to talk to Walter Stein again as long as I live." It's a black, humid day, there's no movement of the dense air through the open windows. My head is pounding.

"Maybe you don't, but the best thing is to be friendly and polite. Let him think you don't care. That almost always works."

"Works?" I am curious in spite of myself. The first drops of rain spatter the green sill.

"Well, if you show you're happy and uncaring — the uncaring part is very important — in spite of him, then he'll want to be *your* friend. It never fails. Then you can decide what you really want." A jag of lightning splits the sky. I cringe, waiting for the earsplitting crash. I'm not disappointed — the ancient walls of the château tremble. Even the radio girls glance up.

"I already know what I want. I never, ever, want to be friends with Walter Stein again." But the words ring as hollow as Nazi propaganda, and Inge grins her triumph. Though I'm probably better off without Walter's tempestuous friendship, without waiting for a sudden ugly mood to sweep across his face like a thundercloud, I adore him. He's my big brother, my almost father, my best-in-the-world friend, and I miss being his confidante, his ally, his little sister-pal. The sad truth is that I'll take whatever he offers. There's no one else left. I need him.

Noah's Ark. That's what we're going to do and we've already begun to rehearse. Inge hopes it will bring us together. Karl, who came up with the idea, is Noah.

"This castle really is like Noah's Ark," he says, "floating us through the war."

Eva the fox smiles coquettishly at him. Why not? Blond and handsome, with velvety-brown eyes, he makes most of the other boys look like scarecrows.

Manfred is to be a panther, which suits him, Inge a lion, and Walter, for unfathomable reasons of his own, has decided to be an elephant. Of course, I'm typecast as the mouse. The other actors roared the first time I came on stage (a chalked-off square in the dining room) and squeaked, "I'm so tiny I have to hop on Giraffe's head to see over the deck rails." I guess they laughed because I'm not tiny at all. Or maybe because I have pink cardboard ears, woolly whiskers and a long, stringy tail. A chicken, a horse, a tiger and a dromedary whose hump keeps slipping, round out the cast. No two by two for our play — this is the war-rations version of Noah's Ark.

Still unable to speak to Walter, I stand as close to him as possible whenever we're both on stage. There's a comfort to his presence, an aura of Walter-ness that envelops and calms me. I go to my bed at night and imagine long conversations — about the play, about our missing families, about ourselves. It's almost as if we're talking again, and talking as I've never dared to before.

"I love you," I whisper into the dark.

"I love you, too, Mouse," Walter whispers back in my mind.

"What made you want to be an elephant?"

"Elephants are big to Mouse's small; they're clumsy and very sociable …"

"That doesn't sound like you at all. Except for the clumsy bit."

He's getting annoyed. "Of course it does, Mouse. I'm the most sociable person I know. And before you contradict me again, elephants also like to play percussion instruments. It's a well-known fact."

I'm not going to argue. The real Walter, annoyed or not, would never say anything half as ludicrous.

The play is a good thing, on the whole — except for Walter and me; we're not talking to each other — but Madame Malheur doesn't think so. She pops in during a rehearsal just in time to hear Karl say that all the animals are to fold their sheets with hospital corners and must dust and sweep their sleeping spaces every day. Her single eyebrow dips in the middle. Are we making fun of her?

"Don't you have anything useful to do?" she asks sourly, glaring at Walter, who's horsing around — if an elephant can — with a length of tatty hose that's supposed to be his trunk. Swallowing hard, he drops the hose, sits in a corner, takes out one of his bits of paper and starts to scribble numbers.

"This play or whatever you call it is a waste of everyone's time. You should be working." Madame swishes away down the corridor, ignoring our sullen faces.

"Hitler," Walter hisses, very, very quietly.

"Come on, Walter. We're going to ignore her, and we can't do this thing without an elephant," Inge implores, her little black lion's nose wiggling as she speaks.

He hesitates, his eyes a strange dense umber, before suddenly springing up. "Elephant will always come back for Lion," he grins, picking up his trunk. Ugh. I've made a huge mistake. He isn't missing our friendship the tiniest bit.

"Let's *all* come back and give it our best, people." Inge cleverly sidesteps his unmistakable message. "Last rehearsal before the big night — well, afternoon."

Later, I wash my face while trying to avoid seeing its pudginess in the mirror. Why can't I be Inge? Clever and beautiful, always knowing the correct thing to say.

Walter's almost irresistibly drawn to lovely creatures —
Eva, Inge — he's a helpless moth to their flame. He would
adore me, too, if I were pretty. I growl despairingly, baring
my teeth, including the bottom crooked one, at my enemy
the mirror, and yank on my nightgown.

"I'm big and fat," I say, which is my usual good-night
to myself. "I'll always be big and fat — and ugly."

"Here we go again," says a muffled voice. It might be
Lisel. "Enough whining, Mouse Girl."

I shut up and climb into bed.

Chapter Eighteen

I'm afraid of making a fool of myself, terrified I'll forget my lines. I go through them over and over on the morning of the performance. There's one that really bothers me: "That's much too difficult for a mouse." I'm supposed to say it when Elephant invites me to help him with the sums he's doing to determine how long we've been at sea. I'm never able to look at Walter while I speak that horrid sentence, and he never looks at me. I once tried leaving it out, but everyone got muddled and skipped two scenes ahead. What a pair — him thin as a fence post, me round as a barrel — speaking in murmurs and looking anywhere but at each other, as if to avoid disease.

It's a hot, hot day in late August. Sweat pours in a steady stream from my armpits to my waist. Madame Malheur, who looks twice as broiling as I feel, keeps pushing back her stringy graying hair. She gave in about the play after an argument with Rose, which we all heard although it was behind a closed door. Rose complained loudly of her usual exhaustion and threatened to quit if the discipline of our lives wasn't loosened.

The directrice slammed out, muttering nasty words and almost knocking over Lisel, who was listening at the keyhole. But, suddenly deciding that the play is good for morale, Madame Malheur has brought all the littler children to the performance, marshaling them in rows. They sit cross-legged on the floor, quiet, their expectant faces turned toward the makeshift stage.

A whisper suddenly goes round the cast. "They're rounding up the Jews." Who is? Which Jews? The rotten-apples-in-the-barrel Jews? Are there any left? I'm not sure I've heard aright and can't deal with the information anyhow. The radio clique has started such rumors before. Once they even told us that the war was over, then laughed as we leapt up and down with delight. I tuck the message in the back of my mind and draw an imaginary blanket over it. I'm nervous enough as it is.

We're all wearing signs so the audience knows for sure what animals we are. The signs look really stupid, in big red lettering so even the tinies can read them. I stand with the others in the wings, a sheet full of holes, through which we squint — and sweat — as Karl muffs his opening lines. The damp stains are spreading on my blouse so I decide not to raise my arms, not even when all the animals are supposed to wave to the audience at the end. Karl, unfortunately, seems to have set the tone of the show. My mouth is parched. It's going to make clicking sounds when I speak, I'm not going to be able to get the words out, I just know it.

The elephant's sign knocks against me, and I spring away, as if seared. He doesn't notice. He notices nothing to do with me.

"Stupid Elephant," I mutter angrily.

"What?" His eyes focus hard on my face, as if I'm a piece of his numerology.

I blush. "Nothing. I was just ... practicing my lines."

"Too late for that. We're on." He gives me a bit of a push and I trip, almost falling over the trailing edge of the sheet, before lumbering across the stage. I'm still blushing, still sweating. The audience titters to see such a fat, damp, overgrown mouse with such ridiculously little ears, but I hardly notice. Walter has spoken to me, touched me. Our miserable exchange has lit a tiny, desperate fire in my brain.

He is speaking now, his voice higher than usual. Perhaps he's nervous, too. "Rather a wet day for a cruise, don't you think?"

The audience guffaws, either on account of his lines, or because anything less resembling an elephant would be hard to imagine. He swishes his trunk and pirouettes. He takes a bow and the audience claps loudly. A new, funny Walter emerged during rehearsals, and he's even funnier in performance. The others love it, are beginning to love him. I'm jealous. I'll have to be funny, too.

Fox says a line, Giraffe follows and finally it's my turn. I open my mouth but nothing comes out. My fingers knot together. The entire world is staring at me. Finally I manage to stutter, in a squeaky voice, which is really quite apt: "What a p-p-pity. I seem to have forgotten my bathing suit."

As the little children giggle, I heave a gusty sigh of relief, but now my stupid tail falls off. I stare at it, uncertain of what to do, then try to ignore the coil of string in the middle of the stage.

"You seem to have lost something, Mouse," Elephant improvises, bending down, picking up the tail and handing it to me with a flourish. Knowing I have to do something —

I can't stuff it in a pocket or dangle it from my hand for an hour — I fumble it back on. I have to contort because my backside seems so far away from the rest of me.

"My bottom seems to have escaped me," I say, so loudly I almost make myself jump. Hoots from the audience. Elephant is beaming. Even Madame Malheur has a sour grin on her ratty face, and her eyebrow has relaxed. I can't help it, I smile. Then I bow like Elephant did and, swiveling my hips, swing my mouse tail round in circles. Everyone howls — some of the littler children go purple in the face.

"Hurray for the mouse!" someone yells.

The laughter suddenly falters and dies, like a bonfire going out. The audience can hear something the actors can't and are concentrating on the double doors at the end of the room. We stare, too, although we don't know why. Fox doesn't say her next line, just stands with her mouth open.

There's a moment's pause — a tremor, almost, of silence. Then both doors push open slowly, like moth wings unfolding. Everyone who lives in the castle is already in this room. I shudder, my teeth clamped tightly together. "They're rounding up the Jews," ran the rumor. "Rounding up the Jews." Is this how Papa felt? How Mama and Josef felt? Were they the rotten apples in the barrel?

I push the thoughts away, but in an instant, huge men in dark uniforms stream in and surround the stage. My mind won't accept what's happening. Instead, I wonder, stupidly, if it's something to do with the play, something that Karl or Rose or even Madame Malheur has dreamed up. Perhaps these men are actors, too. But a stink of fear is coming off the other players, and I can't fool myself any longer. It's the

Vichy police, who do the dirty work for Hitler.

My legs buckle, and I half fall against Manfred, who puts his arm around me.

"Stop right there, *children,* if you'd be so kind." The voice, rich with irony, belongs to a man with enormous, powerful hands. He twists them around a club.

Madame Malheur immediately steps forward.

"I am the directrice," she states haughtily, her nose so high she can barely see over it. She's as tall as he is, and her eyebrow is fierce enough to demolish the entire German army, never mind a few French policemen. But her head's shaking, and that gives her away. "Anything you have to say should be said to me privately."

"Thank you, madame, but that won't be necessary." He snaps his fingers at his comrades and moves closer to us actors. I gaze up into a face covered with little brown moles, beard stubble and snaky nasal veins. The eyes are black and cold, the lips a tight, thin streak. They open again, revealing a gold front tooth.

"All Jews aged sixteen and over are hereby arrested. You have ten minutes to gather your belongings." There's garlic on his breath. That's all I can think of — he's come to arrest us with garlic on his teeth and on his tongue and in his stomach.

"Did you enjoy the sausage?" his wife no doubt asked him an hour or so ago.

"It was delicious, as always."

"Would you like dessert?"

"Maybe later, wife. First I must go out and round up some Jews."

I almost giggle, then gag. I burn with cold. How will I

get myself to my dormitory to pack? There's no point. We won't need clothes where we're going.

Rose dashes forward, looking incredibly ferocious. "Where are you taking them?" she yells, waving her work-stained hands in the air. "They're only children."

"Big children," the policeman says impassively.

Madame Malheur, still trembling, begins to shout too. "But children, nevertheless, and they are under my protection and that of the Swiss Red Cross. I forbid you to remove them."

"Forbid, madame? I'm afraid you still do not realize who is in charge here." He turns back to us. "Go and change, Jews. Fetch your things. Get along, little Mouse."

He smiles kindly, his tooth glinting, and I relax a little. Suddenly he smashes his club against my calf. It's so undeserved, so unexpected, that I cry out and fall, almost downing Manfred. Humiliated, terrorized, I half crawl, half run from the dining hall. The other actors, waxy-faced and terrified, bolt too. When we reach the corridor, afraid to commiserate or even to touch, we hear Madame Malheur through the double doors. She's still arguing, clearly to little avail.

Someone is weeping noisily. I realize with shock that it's me. "We could try escaping," I sniff.

"I'm sure the doors are guarded," Karl replies in a low voice, his face down, in shadow. He is speaking German.

"Through a window ...?"

"*Gott im Himmel,*" Walter snaps, his eyes red with rage. "Don't be so damned stupid, Esther. Can't you hear those trucks outside? We're finished."

Eva screams, a throaty, blood-chilling scream, but for once no one rushes to her rescue. As we drag ourselves up the stairs to the dorms, a policeman tweaks Inge's little black lion nose. "Get going, zoo crew." He grins. Lisel vomits over the banister.

Chapter Nineteen

Twin girls sleep in a bunk not far from mine. They were on the refugee ship *St. Louis* as it sailed around the Americas, searching for a country willing to take a boatload of German Jews. None would. In the end, the ship had sailed back to Europe, and France took the two girls in. They must have felt safe, saved, until they were brought here to Vernet. Now everyone in this camp, including all of us from La Blaize, is about to start that final, one-way journey. We can't fool ourselves — we're being *sent east*. And with a high electric fence, guard towers, searchlights and soldiers with rifles, there's no possibility of escape. Railway tracks run right by our huts. The train will collect us soon. They say that no one leaves Vernet except by cattle car.

Tall, very slim and dressed in black, the twins seem almost one. They're physically and emotionally entwined, spoke only to each other when we arrived, as though no one else existed. They stare through people. It's bad enough to be ignored by one person. Being ignored by two is intimidating. Like mermaids, they glance often in the small mirrors they've brought, brushing each other's long tawny hair till it gleams in the ragged light of the hut. I envy them for their willowy beauty, their luck in having each other. Walter is instantly entranced by them.

There are several long barracks in Vernet for men, mostly political prisoners, and one for Jewish women and children. The boys from La Blaize stay with us and occupy the bunks next to the twins. Walter looks amazingly like them, and has somehow insinuated himself into the girls' magical and mysterious company. He has become their triplet.

Leaning toward one another like lofty flowers, speaking low and musically, the three are inseparable. I've never seen Walter so enmeshed, so graceful, so sadly alive. All the anger has flowed out of him: he belongs.

I never belong. Inge the brave, the foolhardy, has retreated into herself, and little Katerina, who often clung to me, is still at La Blaize, too young to be arrested. When we go east, to our deaths, *I* go alone.

The lights are on all night in the barracks. People are groaning and crying, and I can't sleep. I'm too miserable, and the sounds of anguish make me feel worse. What will happen to us? When will we be taken? Where? I have heard the words "concentration camp." I have heard the terrible, grotesque rumors. My mind won't accept them but won't let them go.

Inge lies next to me, also awake. She huddles in blankets, although it's hot and damp. Only her face shows. She's staring at the ceiling.

"Inge?"

"Shh. I don't want to talk." Shifting onto her side, so she's facing away from me, she sighs and coughs.

"But …"

"Shut up!"

I understand what's happened. She's given up. There's no possibility of escape, no room for bravery. Her hopelessness frightens me more than anything.

I can't see Walter from my bunk, though I imagine that seeing him apart from the ocean-eyed twins might calm me. I sit up, spy a long scarp of blanket in his bunk and lie down again. It's Walter, all right, sleeping next to Manfred, his sharp outline ridged against the covers. His back, curled like that of a small child, looks defenseless, sad, but he's no longer my Walter. Probably never was. I want to cry but I'm dry clear through to my brain.

By morning my eyes are gritty and burning, my mouth tastes foul and there's a heaviness in my stomach. I'm desperate to get to the toilets, a row of holes behind the barracks. We've been given rotten fruit — leftovers from the local harvest — and I have diarrhea.

When I come back from the latrines, not feeling much better, Madame Malheur is in the hut. Everyone from La Blaize is gathered around her. No one cares about her single eyebrow or strictness, no one calls her Hitler. She has suddenly become our only link to the everyday world. A long, gray tendril, escaped from her bun, flops up and down as she speaks.

"We're going to get you out of here, never fear. Whatever you do, don't you dare lose hope."

There's a babble of response, most of it negative. She's been wrong before.

"I'm working with the Red Cross, and they're speaking

to the Germans and the Vichy government. Threatening them, really. You will all be coming back to La Blaize with me. We *will* get things sorted out." She speaks quietly yet vehemently. I stare in fascination at her faint mustache of sharp hair slivers. The hairs must have been shaved. Now they're growing out and make her seem somehow vulnerable.

I try to concentrate. It's hard not to believe her — she sounds so sure of herself. But I already imagine myself in Auschwitz, which I've been told by a political prisoner, Enrico, is where we're headed.

"What about the others?" asks Walter, his yellow eyes narrow as a hawk's.

"What others?"

"The others in the camp — some are no older than we are, some even younger."

"I am so sorry, Walter. I cannot."

Walter has already turned away, moving silently into the orbit of the twins. They make a sorrowful tableau, fingers intertwined and pale oval faces downcast. They look like an engraving from one of Walter's books on the Knights Templar. Even I am curiously moved by their sad, black-clad thinness, their air of hushed doom. The girls' hair falls to their waists, enveloping them and Walter in a dull golden cloak. The three of them are daunting yet beautiful, a piece of Walter's gematria, unfathomable, remote.

After Madame leaves, I watch them furtively. I can never be a part of what they are — I'd bend their mystical triangle out of shape. But the thought that the twins will soon be separated from Walter brings me no ease. Perhaps all of us will be going east. Crushed in the cattle cars to Auschwitz together. Dying together. That will be a kind of belonging, I suppose.

It is half light on September 1. The commandant is in our barracks, surrounded by burly henchmen. They smell of violence.

"All Jews are hereby ordered to pack their suitcases and wait on the platform. As their names are called, they are to board the train."

We have seen nothing further of Madame, so we pack. My hands are numb, judder as I fold my dress, thin as paper, my nightie, two pairs of socks. I stare at my clothes for a long time before shutting the case. Why do I need them? I no longer understand. I clamp my teeth so I don't scream.

Where is Walter? He is with the twins. I drag Inge out of bed and help her pack. We move as though under water, swim-walk outside.

It's hot and dusty. Filth clogs my throat. Names are called. Women trail their children, their luggage. A courtly soldier helps the twins into the first car, careful of their fragile beauty. Now I know their names: Sarah and Leah Grossman.

The day is just beginning, yet everyone is exhausted. I can barely stand. Someone leans against me — it is Eva. The soldiers slide the train doors shut with a clang. The La Blaize group is still on the platform. I am so tired. I just want to lie down.

Suddenly Walter rushes to the first car and claws at the doors. "Let me on," he screams. "I want to go, too."

The courtly soldier smashes him in the back with the butt of his rifle. Walter slams to the ground. "Soon enough, Jew," the soldier says, turning Walter over with his foot and grinning down at him. "Soon enough."

A week later we are back at La Blaize, though life seems very precarious. Our world could be shaken apart again at any time. For now, we've returned to our dormitories, our schooling, our routines, although some of us spend hours arguing: Should we go? Should we stay? The radio people listen to their radio, taking care not to report back. I imagine Nazis or the police waiting just outside the door.

When I fall asleep, which is seldom, I dream of mermaids with flowing golden hair, of women with suitcases, of soldiers, babies. A train leaves a dismal station, breathing angry steam. "Wait for me, wait for me," I scream. "I'm a Jew, too." I frantically run after it, trying to climb aboard as it plunges into the sea.

I wake up gasping, trying to grab hold of the present. But I feel only despair. I have no one. I work in the house, in the yard, in the laundry, shutting memory and fear out as well as I can.

I'm cleaning a dormitory one day when Walter comes around a corner reading. He's still limping a little from his encounter with the soldier. Noticing nothing, as usual, he bumps right into me.

"Hello, Mouse." He smiles sadly, picking up his book.

"Elephant just about knocked you over."

"Elephant." I hardly dare to raise my voice above a whisper in case it shatters the fragile spell. "I've missed you."

"Hug me, Mouse. No one but you touches me." And then, just like that, he's in my arms. I think he's crying.

"I'm sorry about the twins, El, I really am," I murmur into his shoulder.

"They're gone, Mouse. Everyone was taken off the train and shot, didn't even make it to Auschwitz."

"Why are you saying such awful things? You can't know." My voice is staccato, accusatory.

"Oh, but I do, Mouse. Last night, when the others were asleep, I stole the radio: it's all over the news."

"You'll get into trouble," I mutter, aghast at that, too.

"No I won't. I've just committed the perfect crime. They'd be afraid to do anything to me because they shouldn't have had a radio in the first place and Madame might find out. Besides, it's such a little thing compared to ..." Tears glitter at the corners of his eyes.

"Eleph ..."

"I'll put the radio back, Mouse, don't worry. They'll probably never even notice it's been missing. Besides, I don't want to hear any more."

Chapter Twenty

The Vichy government has crumbled. Nazi soldiers are everywhere. One freezing night in December, two members of the Gestapo come to the door demanding that all young men over eighteen be handed over. Lisel and I, who've been straining over the banisters to hear what's going on, dash into the boys' second-floor dormitory.

"Get out," I cry, collapsing onto Walter's bed and waving my arms in a frenzy.

"What is it, Mouse?" He's still half asleep, hair tousled, voice cracking with irritation. "Go away and stop bothering me."

"The Gestapo has come for you — for all the older boys. Get up, get out."

He's out of bed in an instant. Rousing the others, he dashes for the window.

"We'll have to hide on the ledge till they've gone." He pushes Manfred and several of the others through. Then, lithe and silent, he, too, is out, his dear, thin back bent almost double. I imagine all of them spread-eagled against the wall.

"Hurry," Lisel hisses at the remaining boys.

"Are you crazy? I'm not going out there," Karl protests.

"We could fall and kill ourselves." He makes for the stairs, trying for the tower.

"Not that way," Lisel hisses again as she pulls the window closed and locks it. "You'll get trapped."

But it's too late. He and Peter have already gone. We run from the room as the Gestapo men lunge up the stone steps, their guns drawn. There is shouting, the sound of a scuffle. Cornered at the top of the tower, Karl and Peter are brought downstairs and driven away. I sit on the stairs and howl.

Somewhat later, I remember the boys outside. As dawn is breaking, gray and dismal, I unlock the window to tell Walter and the others it's safe. The window catches Walter's kneecap. He doesn't fall, he flies, as I did that dreadful night when I broke my wrist. But *he* flies backwards, yelling "*Gott im Himmel*" with a high, keening shout.

Then, "Stupid Mouse," Walter mutters as he hits the frozen grass. One of his legs sticks out askew, a puppet's leg. A piece of falling plaster strikes his face. He twists a little, lies still. It begins to snow.

Walter has broken his arm and his hip — a clean break through the femur — and the plaster fractured his nose. He's in agony, and it's all my fault.

"No, it's not, Mouse." He speaks slowly, valiantly, through his teeth. Every breath, every word, is anguish. "If it weren't for you … I'd be in Auschwitz."

We're in the second cellar, Walter on a makeshift bed.

All the older boys are down here now, in case the Gestapo comes back. They live in candlelight, sleep on straw with the insects and rats. But it's a good hiding place — through a trap door under the wine cellar — and little enough discomfort to pay for their lives.

Walter and I sit silently, but I know what he's thinking because I'm thinking it too. Karl and Peter haven't come back, probably never will. Madame threatened and cajoled, she offered gasoline, which the Red Cross has and the Nazis need. But in the end she could do nothing. The boys made one wrong choice — to go up rather than out — and now they're gone.

Brown water drips in a corner, a regular pinging noise.

"It'll happen to all of us if we don't get away from here," I whisper. Manfred glances over, as if curious to know what we're talking about.

"Right." Walter grins wryly, more of a grimace, really, and holds up his arm, which is splinted and bandaged. The village doctor did it. We trust him.

"I realize you can't go now, Eleph," I say. "You have to mend first. But I'll wait for you and then we'll go together. Some have already gone."

"With false papers … I know. It'll be your turn next, little Mouse. Madame told me … she was sending you … with Naomi and Eva and Manfred … to cross into Switzerland."

"Just let her try." I am close to crying, almost shouting. "I won't go anywhere without you, Walter."

"Shh. You'll do as you're told. You can't wait … it's too dangerous. Even for a girl."

"I know. That was the mistake my mother made.

She always thought the Nazis would only take the men."

"Sorry ... I'm sorry." Closing his eyes, he winces slightly and tries to move into a more comfortable position. I pile more straw under his pillow, but it doesn't help. His leg is heavily bound, and his nose is crooked and still somewhat swollen.

"Elephant will follow Mouse, just as soon as he's better," he says at last, with great effort. "Mouse is his ... best friend. Elephant wouldn't ... abandon Mouse ... for the world."

He talks this way now when he has something intimate to say. I answer him in kind, hardly able to contain the emotion that has saturated our friendship since Vernet. I don't feel fat or ugly when we talk so. Elephant and Mouse can speak the thoughts and feelings Walter and Esther would never have the courage to declare.

I squeeze his good hand, and he smiles up at me, amber eyes deep in their yellowish, bruised sockets.

"Mouse will wait for Elephant," I say firmly.

But Mouse doesn't wait. Madame has other plans and sends her away.

I leave Walter a card. *In the event of an accident, call Mouse.*

"Put it in your wallet," I nag, like a bossy mother.

"Shouldn't it say, 'In the event of *another* accident'?" Walter grins, his mouth full of bread, his lap full of the gematria he's working on. His bruises have faded, and his arm is mostly healed; but he still can't walk, and the doctor has warned him that if he takes it too fast, he'll ruin his hip for life.

"You won't really be able to call me," I say, feeling sorry for myself. "I don't even know where I'll be. It's just to remember me by."

"I'll find you, no matter where you are. Just squeak and I'll be there. One day Mouse will sleep curled up in Elephant's ear." He thrusts the card deep into his pocket.

I try to smile, but a vision of his body lying in a gutter plays on the inside of my eyelids.

Even with my eyes open, I don't see him the way he is, skinny, wounded, intensely human. He's become remote, already enveloped in the cold haze of memory, like my family.

"Elephant refuses to imagine life without Mouse," Walter insists.

"Even so …"

"Don't say it, silly Mouse," he warns, perhaps rightly.

We hug. He touches his lips to mine, and I taste bread and salt.

"Go away." He shoves his hand against my shoulder, his fingers jabbing through my thin blouse as though I'm suffocating him. "You're keeping me from my work. Go away." He picks up his pencil and writes rapidly.

"Good-bye," I whisper, dismayed. There's no response. His growing columns of numbers are the final humiliation. Mortified, I pick up my case and walk away as briskly as I can. I meet up with Eva, Naomi and Manfred, but carry the briny taste of Walter's kiss, or perhaps of my tears, all the way to the station.

Chapter Twenty-one

I am now Nicole Chausson, though the papers to prove it haven't come through from the Jewish Underground. We will have to be very careful, all four of us, to elude the Nazis and reach the house where we've been told we may find help. "May," not "will."

Esther Wilinski has disappeared. She climbed onto this train, dragging her shabby suitcase, but Nicole Chausson climbs off in Lyon. The suitcase feels light now — funny how it used to be so heavy. All that work must have built muscles.

I keep forgetting my name. It doesn't sound like me at all, and I'm afraid I might not respond if someone speaks or calls to me. Nicole looks remarkably like Esther, though. She's *zaftig,* scared, lonely. Especially lonely, without Walter. She wears a coat that is much too tight across her breasts, but surprisingly baggy at the waist and hips, and scuffed, scabby shoes. I would prefer her beautiful, well-dressed and confident, but, new name or not, I am still Esther/Mouse, in the coat and shoes I left Germany in ages ago. I'm so tired of myself.

"Eva?" I ask, as we toil up an unfamiliar hill toward the town. "Do you think —?"

Eva halts. We all halt with her. "Thérèse, idiot. My

name is Thérèse." These are her first words to me since we left La Blaize.

"Sorry."

"I should think so." Eva rolls her eyes at Naomi, now Bernadette. "My feet are killing me."

"Mine, too. Could do with a new pair of boots. Only the laces are holding these together." Naomi/Bernadette stares down at her feet and scowls. "Think of all the gorgeous shoes I had before the war. Beautiful white stockings, too."

I've already forgotten what I wanted to say to Eva. It couldn't have been important. We're in the most dangerous situation of our lives, but Eva is still the sun, with Naomi and Manfred revolving around her. Lost, millions of miles away, spins Esther/Mouse/Nicole, the outermost planet. My orbit is so immense I feel I'm traveling in a straight line away from them.

Although she called a temporary truce at Vernet — she leaned on me and even thanked me after our ordeal — Eva's become nastier than ever since I've been friendly with Walter again. She doesn't want him herself — he's far too clumsy and self-absorbed — but she can't bear anyone else to have his attention. Or rather, she can't bear that he might want someone else more than he wants her. It doesn't matter that Walter's nowhere near enough to be of any use to either of us. She's still possessive. She'd have gloated had she seen him shove me away. As it is, she's furious that she has to put up with me — she's only technically on my side of the war.

"I can't understand why Madame didn't send Lisel with us — or even Inge — instead of that stupid ... what's her name? … Nicole." Eva pulls her woolen mitten more firmly over her left hand and splays her fingers. It's as if I'm not here.

"You know Inge left last week to try to get to Spain." Manfred's hands are in his pockets because he doesn't have gloves, and his teeth are chattering. "She says she'll stop on the way if she can get work with the Underground, the Maquis."

"Right," sneers Naomi. "Just the job for a girl."

"Walter didn't even say *au revoir* to me." I feel so deathly tired I don't even attempt to hide my feelings. "I said good-bye, but he turned away."

Eva manages a snigger that infuriates me. Better mad than hopeless, I suppose. Naomi/Bernadette is staring at her boots again as though they belong to someone else. She has one black lace, knotted in several places, and one brown one.

"Disgusting," she finally mutters. I'm not sure whether she's talking about Inge, or Walter, or me, or the state of her footwear.

"We have to pull together on this —" Manfred says, gazing at a distant cluster of houses so as not to be seen to be challenging Eva, "— or we're done for."

It's beginning to snow — hard, white lumps like the sugar Papa held between his teeth when he drank tea. Eva is still whining about me, as if I'm a shabby old hat she'd like to throw in the trash. I bite hard on my lip to keep from shouting at her. It wouldn't do any good and would draw attention to us. I try to convince myself she's doing this because she's scared and I'm a convenient target. Still, I'm ready to belt her. Miserable and cold, we straggle up to the top of the hill. But all the bad feeling, the squabbling, has affected our concentration. We don't even notice when two Nazi soldiers, who must have followed us from the station, come up behind us.

"*Guten Tag,*" says the younger one, who looks no older than Manfred. I'm so shocked to see him I almost drop my suitcase. "Papers, please."

Eva smiles at him. "Good evening, sir. Freezing cold night, isn't it?"

"Your papers," he repeats, unmoved by her charm.

Of course, we have no papers, or none that we can show, anyhow. We hem and haw and give all sorts of excuses; we tell them our new names over and over and pretend we come from Paris, but it doesn't make the slightest difference. Our adventure is over.

"How could we have been so stupid?" says Manfred, as soon as we're shut into a tiny room in Gestapo head-quarters. One dim and dusty lightbulb casts its miserable light upon us. "How could we have thought we could get away without identification papers?"

"Why did Madame let us go like this?" complains Eva. "Without even a story to say where we're from?"

"She must have been pushed for time," I suggest. "She wanted to get as many of us away as possible before the Nazis came back."

Naomi says nothing, just sits on a chair in the corner and removes her boots. She touches a chilblain and moans softly.

Eva ignores me. "How come you told them we're Jewish?" she demands of Manfred, with an accusatory stare.

"I didn't. They found out."

"How?"

"Oh, think, Eva. When they separated us, they checked me over."

"Checked what? How could that prove anything?"

Manfred turns crimson all the way up to his hairline.

"Eva, *come on*. Jewish boys look different ... down there." Naomi, irritated beyond belief, has spoken at last. "Don't act stupider than you are."

"So we can also thank Madame for sending us with a *circumcised* boy," Eva snarls. "We'd have been all right on our own. Jewish *girls* look just like everyone else. I've been told I look very Aryan."

"Much good that will do you," Naomi snaps.

"Esther or Nicole or whatever her stupid name is — she looks Jewish. Couldn't be anything else. Comes from having eaten too much *chaleh* from Papa's bakery. She'd have given us away even if Manfred didn't."

"Don't be ridiculous," says Manfred.

I catch Eva's grimace, but I'm barely listening. While they've been arguing, I've noticed a window, high in the slope of the outside wall. I stare at it from all angles, weighing the odds, before making my proposal.

"Listen, we could escape through there. It'll be tight for me, but you others should make it easily."

"Are you out of your mind? We're on the second floor. We'd kill ourselves," Eva almost shrieks. "Or get torn to shreds by bloodthirsty dogs when we hit the ground."

"You sound just like Karl," I say bitterly.

"I don't want to die jumping out a window."

"You're going to die if you stay here. We all are. Remember the train to Auschwitz? Remember how you had to lean on me for support just thinking of it?"

"I wouldn't touch you with a barge pole."

"You weren't so brave — or nasty — back then."

Eva glares at the wall. I want to whack her cheek hard with my hand, to scream at her to stop hurting me and see sense, but I know she has to have someone to hate. It's nothing personal. It's just the way she is. That's what I keep telling myself, anyway.

"Madame will rescue us. She always does," Naomi says flatly, rejoining what looks like the winning team.

"Don't be silly," I groan. "She couldn't rescue Karl. Or Peter. How will she even know we're here?"

"Don't say that!" Naomi turns away, too.

Manfred doesn't say a word, but after a minute he shakes his head slowly — no, and no again.

"It's too risky," he mutters finally, as if the words are a great heaviness.

"This isn't a parlor game — we don't get to start life again if we lose." My mouth tastes so bitter I can barely get the words out.

"Shut up," Eva says sharply. And that's the end of my escape plan.

No. Not quite the end, because when the light's off and we lie down to sleep, I think about Inge, about how brave she can be, despite her gloom in Vernet. I remember how she climbed into our train compartment in Germany, pretending to be one of us, to escape. I see her now as she was that first day, tall and graceful and daring.

Well, if she can be brave, so can I. The little window dances in front of my eyes. I'm not certain I can wriggle through it or jump without severely hurting myself. But

Lynne Kositsky

there's one thing I *am* sure of — I don't want to die, at least not without a fight. And staying here, going wherever the Nazis send us, is death. I have to try, even if there's only the tiniest chance I'll survive. I also have a desperate, unscratchable itch to leap through that window.

So as soon as everyone's either asleep or pretending to be, I creep across the room and anchor a chair beneath the window. Then I clamber on. My weight causes it to groan, and a chair leg scrapes outward, making a ghastly chalk-on-blackboard screech against the stone floor. Nobody stirs. I almost hope Manfred might — I want him to come with me.

"Manfred?" I whisper. There's no response.

The window's bigger than I thought. It's hard to open, but I've had some practice with handles and sashes, and window fittings in general. They're my stock in trade, you might say. I can make it easily as long as I don't wear my coat.

I stand on the chair for several minutes, wondering if I dare jump and whether it's forgivable to leave the others. The thought of abandoning Manfred is more sickening each second. He's never done me any harm — he just defended me against Eva. But then I see the moon swinging high in the purple sky, a slick cream sliver. That delicate crescent is life — and my only hope that one day I might meet up with Walter again.

I glance back. Eva's lying crookedly along the bunk. For a moment I think her eyes are open and staring at me, but I soon realize it's a trick of moonlight and shadow. Naomi lies next to her, her right arm flung out, fingernails gleaming in the pale moon's beam. Manfred, on the bunk

112

above, is entirely covered by blanket, and I'm almost grateful I can't see his face.

But how can I leave him? He didn't sound at all sure he wanted to stay. If I could just persuade him, it might redeem me, justify my decision.

"Manfred?" My voice is urgent this time. I imagine I catch the sound of a sob, listen intently but hear nothing further except my own pulse hammering in my ears.

I am suddenly angry. It's their own fault. I offered them a way out, all of them, but they wouldn't take it. They're not my responsibility. I won't ever to try to help anyone again. Except Walter — if I ever get the chance.

One last spasm of guilt, and then, as if of its own accord, my coat sails out of the window. It is my only possession, as the Nazis have taken our suitcases. The coat lands with a gentle sigh on the snowy ground. With barely a pause, I sail out, too.

Chapter Twenty-two

My dearest Eleph,

I'm safe, I should tell you that before I start, so you won't be too alarmed, but I have the most absolutely horrible story to tell you. It started almost as soon as we got off the train. We were captured and imprisoned. The Nazis asked us reams of questions, then shut us in a little cell-like room. I escaped through a window, but the others wouldn't come with me. I didn't fall head first, thank God, or even break a wrist this time, just got a few nasty bruises. Eva, Naomi and Manfred — well, I don't know what happened to them and I feel angry they stayed behind. Maybe I've killed them, sealed their fate, but here I am — in a convent, of all places. I just knocked on the door in the middle of the night and the nuns took me in, no questions asked. I had tried the address we'd been given by Madame Malheur, but the house was all boarded up.

The nuns have been very kind to me and to the other girls here, waifs and strays all of us. We live upstairs, help out and don't ask questions. It's an unwritten rule to be silent about where we come from. But Eleph, this morning the Gestapo came. The Mother Superior can be quite intimidating and wouldn't let them above the ground floor.

We watched from upstairs, quaking. After they'd left, she said that if we had anything to hide, we should leave by morning because they'd be back and she couldn't hold them off forever. So early tomorrow I'm on my way again. The Swiss checkpoint is closed, I've heard, to all but small children, so I'll make for the Spanish border.

This paper and nib pen, and the black inky smell as I write, remind me of the inkwells at La Blaize, of letters I wrote to Berlin. They remind me that I'm still alive and have ink-stains on my fingers to prove it. I'll do my best to stay that way, though with clean hands, of course. For myself. For you. Hope you're not annoyed with me any longer. You were so angry and dismissive at the end because you didn't want me to go. I'm right, aren't I, darling Elephant?

A nun will mail this. Trust it reaches you safely. I thank heaven you weren't with us. God bless you always. There's an emptiness next to me where you should be.

Your still living, ever loving

Mouse xxxxx

Chapter Twenty-three

I'm in a new, strange place. I don't know what to think or how to act. After leaving the convent, I lived in ditches and doorways for several days, getting shabbier and dirtier and colder, becoming desperate and sick with fright, until a tiny woman with a concrete block of a face found me. I don't know what to make of her. She stands in front of me now, asking question after question.

"Name?" she asks matter-of-factly.

What should I answer? Esther Wilinski? Nicole Chausson? Something else? I can't think of one thing I can say that won't damn me. Tears well out of my eyes and down my stupid cheeks.

"No use crying. I suppose you'd like to know *my* name?"

I smile tremulously.

"It's Madame Blanche. Too clean a name for an old rogue like me. Do you have papers?"

I feel myself pale but say nothing.

"How old are you?"

This is easier. I can't see how my age will betray me. "Sixteen."

"You look older," she says, looking me over. "You don't have anything else to wear, do you?"

I shake my head miserably.

"Never mind. I keep a supply for occasions like this. I should have something that will fit. No, don't thank me."

I'm not about to. She'll never have anything that'll slide down over my behind, and I tell her so.

"Nonsense. I'm pretty good at judging size. Now stop fussing." She rummages through a box and holds up a dress that is both ugly and too small. "Try it on," she says.

"It'll never fit." But, amazingly, it does. "Thanks," I say, gracelessly.

The dress is still ugly, and she's still a stranger. Though her kitchen is spotless and reminds me of home, and though she seems kind enough in a busybody way, I have no idea whether I should trust her. She looks me up and down for a moment but says nothing, just hands me two skimpy sweaters and a skirt. Then I'm given bread and wine and a bed to sleep in — a real bed.

A cat has adopted me, a three-legged tabby. He's sleek and relatively well fed, a miracle in these times. Although he won't sit on my lap he rubs himself against and around my legs, his tail flicking up and down. His eyes are the same color as Walter's.

"How on earth did he get in?" Madame asks.

"I'm not sure. He was in my bedroom."

"His name is Chandler. An English soldier hiding here named him — yes, I've had all sorts. Chandler's a magician, an escape artist. His leg was crushed by a Nazi convoy, but I nursed him back to health. I thought this time he'd left for good." After that she treats him like she treats me, in a mostly kind, no-nonsense way. Chandler does have rather a haughty English way about him. He accepts tidbits as though he expects them, climbs up high so he can look down his long nose at us and comes and goes as he pleases.

Late in the evening of my third day, not knowing whether I should stay or leave, or what's expected of me, I hear the sound of a key in the lock. It must be Madame. She's been out for hours. But instead, a tall, thin young man appears, sliding like an eel through the back door. He is sad-eyed and mysterious. His fingers are long and bony, like the chicken feet Mama used to boil in the soup.

"You're Jewish?" he asks.

"What's it to you?" Even in good times, one doesn't give away secrets to strangers.

Sad Eyes taps his foot. "I'm not here to hurt you, and I don't have time for social chitchat."

"Please don't take me away," I beg.

"Silly girl, I'm here to help you. Are you Jewish?"

I finally nod, deciding I have no choice but to trust him.

"We'll have papers made for you and get you a food ration book. In the meantime, Madame will look after you. She's done the same for many of our people."

Faint with relief, I thank him. He goes away without a good-bye. A few nights later he's back, his black scarf wrapped around his nose and mouth, muffling his voice.

"Your name is Solange LeGrand. She left home and disappeared in Rheims a while back. Now you can find yourself a job and get food with your own ration book."

He pulls papers from beneath his coat and drops them on the kitchen table. Chandler examines them as if he's a feline policeman. I want to thank Sad Eyes, but he's already slipped back out into the night.

After he leaves, I cut my regrown hair short with a pair

of nail scissors and dye it blonde. The smell of the bleach makes my eyes water and my chest hurt. When I've finished, my scalp burns, and my fine hair is yellow straw. If I don't brush it down with a little water or oil, it stands up around my head like a brittle halo. I don't like what I've become. For the first time, I want to be me.

"You overdid it," Madame says sourly. "Go easy on the peroxide, Solange. Otherwise, your hair will fall out."

I shudder at the thought of being bald twice in a lifetime. "I'll leave it on for less time if I have to do it again."

"Of course you'll have to do it again. In a month your roots will show. Didn't your mother teach you anything?"

"My mother was sent east, Madame," I say coldly. "I assume she's dead."

"Well." Madame pauses for a moment. "Pluck those dark eyebrows of yours and bleach them, too — but carefully, so you don't damage your eyes."

Taking her advice, her tweezers and her peroxide, I go to work again. Afterwards, my eyes smart, but my newly pale eyebrows are thin, arched lines. My appearance hasn't improved, but it's different. Same flabby face, but lighter eyebrows and, after my second application of bleach, a brittle cap of whitish hair. Sometimes hairs break off like dry twigs as I comb them. I throw them away quickly, frightened at how many might follow.

What would Walter think of me? One night I dream that he passes me on the street without saying hello. I run after him.

"Elephant, it's me," I yell. He turns, stares straight through me with his piercing yellow eyes.

"Don't bother me now, Mouse. I'm off to war. I have to

defeat Hitler," he says and continues on his way.

When I awake, I'm still shouting after him, and Madame is trying to quiet me. "We'll have the *Milice* on us if you keep that up. They can hear you on the street."

For a moment I don't recognize her. All I can feel is the pain of having lost Walter again, even though it's only a dream.

"I'm so lonely," I murmur. "What am I doing here? Everything is so strange."

"Pull yourself together, mademoiselle. There's no room for sentimentality in a war."

"Still, I need my friend. I need kind words. I need comforting, like everybody else."

"If you're lonely, cuddle the cat. Doubtless he's lonely, too." She clucks her tongue and marches back to bed.

I hug Chandler fiercely, kissing his blunt head over and over despite his shrill objections. When I finally put him down, he limps into a corner and glares at me balefully. Then he washes all three paws as though I've contaminated him.

"Cat and Mouse," I whisper to him. "You and I. But will Mouse ever see Elephant, ever again?"

If Chandler knows, he isn't telling. He just leaps on top of a chair back and stares down at me in his superior way. I try to get back to sleep, can't, catch a sudden vivid image of Walter bent over his papers, studying gematria. What's he doing now? Is he asleep? Is it possible he's thinking of me, wondering where I am? I've written to him twice since I've been here, but there's been no reply.

It seems that I'm welcome to stay with Madame, so I've found a job in a shoe factory. The stink of leather permeates everything, and I feel sick by the end of the day. I'm reminded of the smell of my uncle's new car before the war. It was supposed to be a treat, but riding in it I'd feel warmer and stickier every minute till I'd almost suffocate. Eventually my aunt would get him to stop the car so I could stumble out and throw up. Now I walk the mile or so from work every evening, grateful for the fresh air. It clears the horrible odor from my nostrils and the queasiness from my belly.

This evening it's raining, cold. My back aches from bending over the cobbler's last all day. My thin shoes glide over the wet cobbles like ice skates, and I have to take tiny, precise steps to keep my balance. That makes my back worse. Someone is close by, I suddenly realize, very close. Footsteps echo my own on the slick, deserted street.

I stop. Silence. I don't dare turn, start forward again.

A light tap on the arm, and my heart shrinks to the size of a walnut. I swivel, expecting a German soldier. I squint, terrified at what I might see. But it's only the thin Jewish boy, rain dripping from his hat brim pulled low across his gaunt face.

"What are your plans?" he asks. There's never any small talk with him.

"Plans?" I'm surprised at the question, start to gabble. "I like living with Madame Blanche, although it's not home. Nowhere is home anymore. I'd like to get out of France, of course, maybe go to Spain." What an idiot I sound.

He cuts me off. "We helped you, Solange."

"Yes, you did. I'm very grateful." There's something he wants of me.

"Now you will help us. Welcome to the Jewish Underground."

"Just a minute! What — ?" But Sad Eyes is gone.

I'm not brave enough for this.

I'm to be a courier, Madame tells me as she stirs soup. That's what women do in the Underground, and I mustn't mess up. I'm outraged. I haven't chosen this. They've chosen it for me.

"I will mess up, I know I will. I'm clumsy and stupid. I cry too much ... and I'm scared."

"Forget it, Solange. Your clumsiness and occasional stupidity will serve you well. The Nazis will never suspect such a one as you."

"Thanks very much." It's all right for *me* to go on about my shortcomings, but not for her to do it.

"As for fear, it stalks all of us. We move in lockstep with it."

"I suppose so." I'm worried I'll lose my temper and scream out my fear and anger at her. Instead I go to my bedroom, grab the unwilling cat and sob all over his ears. "It's all right for you," I grumble, as he wriggles free and jumps from the floor to the chair to the mantelpiece. "No one expects you to be a hero. No one expects you to save anyone except yourself. And you haven't even done a very good job of that."

He stares down at me, aloof, his irises transparent in the dim room.

"Get out of here," I shout at him, thoroughly fed up.

"Shut up," Madame yells from the kitchen. "Come and have some soup."

Two days later, a small bundle of documents awaits me when I arrive home from work. I leave them sitting on the table while I eat a hasty supper of bread and gruel. Having swallowed the last mouthful and stared at the package for far too long, I pick up the first piece of paper gingerly. I am to deliver the enclosed identities to Jews, much as Sad Eyes delivered mine to me. A separate sheet gives an address and lists their new names. I stare at the names, wondering who might be about to own them. They're like me, trying to survive. I feel a connection, but it's not a good one. I don't want to see them, know them, speak to them. It's a responsibility that weighs me down.

Madame Blanche is out, so I delay. I try to comb my useless blond mop. No matter how much I smooth it down, the back spikes up, so I jam an old hat of Madame's over it. I splash water on my face and onto my palms, but run out of ways to procrastinate. I finally go back into the kitchen and scoop up the documents. I could go away, not deliver them, vanish into the countryside. Madame would come back to an empty house. But I want to stay here. Madame Blanche and Sad Eyes are kind; they make me feel safe, and I suppose this unsafe excursion is repayment. As I tuck the papers inside my coat, each beat of my heart, hard and painful, rocks my chest.

I don't want to leave the house. The smell of candle grease is familiar and comforting. The soup is bubbling quietly on the stove. Stone soup. Madame makes it out of almost nothing. But it's delicious. Chandler is purring because I gave him some tiny dribbles of milk. But I have to go.

When I finally deliver the papers, people grab my hands and murmur their thanks, looking exhausted and nervous. I don't want their gratitude, want nothing to do with them. I almost hate them, am gone as fast as I came, arriving home just before curfew.

My next job, even less welcome, is escorting an old woman to a safe place. She sees a poster of Hitler and starts to yell in Yiddish.

"He stole my children. He took my grandchildren. He killed them all, that devil."

"Shut your mouth," I mutter at her in German. "You'll get us arrested. One more word and I'll leave you here for the Nazis."

"Oy, oy ..." she mumbles through her toothless gums, banging her walking stick on the cobblestones then pointing it waveringly at the poster. "Oy, oy, oy."

Hitler glares down at us. A cold wind blows dust into my eyes.

Gott im Himmel, I want to scream, but, "Be quiet," I hiss, jabbing her arm. My knees are about to give way. "D'you want to get us killed?"

Tears run from her rheumy eyes. "Oy, oy, oy." I gasp, try to recall my grandmother, my *Bubi,* how grateful I'd be if someone saved her. It doesn't help. My grandmother's been dead for years, and I remember only a whiff of lavender and furniture polish. This old woman smells of salami and dirt and mothballs, and she won't shut up. I have an overwhelming urge to hit her.

People are staring. "Forgive my grandmother," I beg them in French. "The war has been too hard on her. She's a bit gone in the head and only remembers her native Dutch."

There are encouraging nods and smiles, and I manage, very slowly and with much prodding, to get the old woman to the safe house. On the way back to Madame's, I collapse against a wall. I could have been arrested. I could be dead — and all for a smelly old woman who means nothing to me. Thank God there were no soldiers around. Thank God no one recognized Yiddish. Thank God I'm alive.

My darling Eleph,

I miss you so much I can't see straight. I need to see you or my heart will break. Nothing in life means anything without your friendship. The days drag by. You're my last link with childhood, with family. I need your bear — no, elephant — hugs so badly to make up for the dangers of every day. The women I work with at the shoe factory think Jews have horns, say the one good thing that Hitler's done is to rid the country of them.

I worry about you day and night, but I'm sure you must be all right. If anything should happen to you, I'd know it in my bones, and then life wouldn't be worth living.

Your loving, still a bit zaftig *Mouse*

P.S. Licks from Chandler

I tear the letter up and throw it into the stove. According to Madame Malheur, who recently wrote to me in cryptic fashion, Walter left La Blaize weeks ago. No one has any idea where he is.

Chapter Twenty-four

I don't want to but can't stop myself. I'm thinking about how I got to France from Belgium. It was horrible, but most of it, except how it ended, is a comfort to me now, because Walter looked after me.

We didn't even know where we were going at first. Like the other girls, I had dragged on almost all my clothes in the time we'd had to pack: three pairs of underwear, two skirts and tops, a heavy sweater and coat. It was wear them or leave them behind. I was sweating and couldn't stand myself — or the horrible boxcar that we'd been packed into. And although I sat on the floor, had already been lulled to sleep several times by the side-to-side motion of the train, I still clasped my little suitcase. In it were a couple of textbooks, a wash bag, a dress, a night-gown, a picture of my family and an extra sweater. An old lipstick of Mama's that I'd taken when I left Germany was tucked down the side of the case. When I felt too miser-able to keep going, I could unscrew it, smell its faint perfume and remember her. It was only a trace of her, but sometimes it was almost enough. I've lost that lipstick now.

One of the counselors had reserved two cars for us, one for the boys and one for the girls, but at the last station we'd gotten mixed up. We'd been on the platform, eating some broth provided by the Red Cross. What a strange bunch of refugees we were: Jewish boys and girls, Belgian nationals and nuns. All fleeing the Germans. The nuns gave us biscuits before returning to their car at the end of the train, their huge hats flapping like sheets on a washing line. Most of the other refugees climbed aboard, as we sat being counted. We were always being counted. Suddenly the train made impatient, throat-clearing noises as if it were about to take off, and our counselors, in a panic, pushed us onto the cars.

Caught in an almost suffocating crush, sad and hot, I heard the familiar *"Gott im Himmel"* and realized that Walter was close by. His voice was a beacon. I crawled toward the sound, dragging my case.

"Walter," I whispered, rather too pathetically.

"Hello, Mouse. Convenient mode of transport, isn't it?"

"Do you know where we're going?"

"South of France, probably, like everyone else. Sit here on the side and lean against me. It'll prop me up, too."

I did as I was told, so that we were nearly, but not quite, back to back. After a while I became bold enough to twist around and lean my head tentatively against his shoulder. Amazingly, he slid his arm around me, drawing me closer, the rough material of his jacket brushing my neck.

"Little, tiny Mouse," he murmured, taking me by surprise.

Enveloped in his warm boy smell, I didn't stir out of his circle of comfort for hours. Now when I'm especially sad I try to recapture the feeling of being surrounded by Walter. I want that more than anything else.

I was asleep when an earsplitting blast lifted the train

and slammed us against the wall of the car.

We crashed back down as the engine halted. There was the stink of burning, a confusion of men's voices, the pounding of boots outside.

"What's happening?" Lisel shrieked. No one knew, no one replied.

Walter's fingers had dug into me so hard I could feel his nails through my many layers of clothing. I glanced down at his white knuckles, but hadn't the courage to tell him he was hurting me.

"We've been bombed, I think," he whispered.

Cold sweat cascaded down my body. My voice seemed to have liquefied, my muscles dissolved. Some of the smaller children started to howl, and in the dimness I could see others trying to console them. Walter scrambled across to a little boy who had gashed his head, took out a handkerchief and mopped up the blood. But I couldn't help anyone. I was paralyzed by fear, until someone outside opened the doors and the even hotter afternoon air rushed in, hazed with smoke.

I suddenly needed to pee badly. It always happens when I am frightened. In the boxcar, you just had to do it in a corner, which no one would with boys around. I crept over to the door and half slid, half fell to the ground, then ran for the bushes on wobbly legs. It wasn't till I was coming back that I really saw and understood.

What was left of the train stood, mostly on the tracks, in the middle of a field. There wasn't a house in sight. The cars booked by the children's home were intact, but the last car was a charred ruin. Smoke poured from the wreckage; an occasional flame spurted along the door. The nuns. It was then that I really knew about war.

Thank God, Walter was alive — we might so easily have been killed. "God bless and keep you, Eleph," I whisper. Will He? I stub out the thought the way Papa ground his cigarette in the big silver-colored ashtray in our apartment.

"Your smoking will be the death of me," Mama used to complain. She was wrong.

Chapter Twenty-five

A Jewish woman in hiding has given birth to twin boys. The mother is sick, and her milk has dried up. The babies' starved cries will soon draw the attention of a nosy neighbor or the Germans. It will mean almost certain death for the three of them, the woman's husband and the gentile couple giving them shelter. Milk is hard to come by, so we've tried giving the infants rags dipped in wine, but they drop off to sleep for a only few moments. Then they wail again.

"Even if there were enough milk, they'd still scream the place down," Sad Eyes remarks gloomily during a meeting at our house. "You know what has to be done." He says it sharply, as if it's a geometry problem. But he still looks wretched and exhausted.

I give Chandler a quick stroke, as much to hide my face as for comfort. I feel sorry for the babies. I might not want to risk my life for them, but I don't want them dead, either. I want them to have a *chance*. The word imprints itself in big red letters on my brain. I think about the twins in Vernet, Leah and Sarah Grossman. Somehow, these tiny infants are a replacement for them. How macabre, I think, that a cat here can be safer than a child.

In the end, it's Madame Blanche who speaks up. "If we kill babies, we're no better than the Nazis."

"If we don't, we're killing everyone in that house. Maybe even ourselves, if the trail leads back to us. The only ethics we can afford are those of necessity." Sad Eyes drapes his muffler around his neck. He wears it even in spring. Perhaps he once wrapped his prayer shawl around his shoulders in much the same way, his hands lingering on the fabric, his face downcast. White bone gleams through the skin of his cheeks, and for a moment he resembles the plaster saints Madame has on her mantel.

"Who will do it?" Madame asks, her face pale. She crosses herself.

"I will. Tomorrow. I'll take Julie with me." Julie's another member of the underground. Sad Eyes has made the wrong decision and I despise him for it.

"Sorry to be the bearer of bad news." His voice is as faint as the print on old newspaper. He slips like an apparition through the back door.

"We have to save those babies," I say, surprising myself. "We can't just let them die."

"Go to bed," warns Madame. "I'm not in the mood to talk." Innocent children get to all of us. She's crying.

It's still dark — the birds aren't singing yet — when Madame tugs me into consciousness. "Get dressed. We have work to do before you go to the factory."

I dive deeper under my blanket. It took me hours to fall asleep, what with worrying about the twins and Walter and myself, and the cat walking all over the bed.

"Put a coat on. There's a strong wind, so button up."

Grumbling, I dress and join her. My stomach is growling. Chandler tries to slip through the door as we leave. "Don't want you out alone, little cat. You can't afford to lose another leg." I shoo him back in.

The streets are forlorn and wintry. Galelike winds buffet us, almost knock us down. Dust and rubbish fly along the gutters. We take a wide detour around a man peeing against the wall of a bakery. The smell of warm bread mixed with his strong urine is sickening. "Too much wine last night," he yells, as if we need to know.

As it grows light, two Nazi soldiers pass us and nod. I look the other way, I don't want anything to do with them, but Madame nods back, holding onto her best Sunday hat and remarking on the harsh weather. Soon we're climbing a steep hill.

"We're near the babies' house."

Madame doesn't reply.

"You're going to strangle them and save Sad Eyes the bother. You two are always dragging me into things."

"Don't be more stupid than you can help, Solange. And stop calling him Sad Eyes. Marcel is a perfectly respectable name."

"I won't kill those babies," I add loudly.

"Do you really think I'd bring you here for that? Come."

Why didn't she tell me straight out? Perhaps she was afraid I'd make a fuss about going against Sad Eyes' orders. In fact, I'm delighted. The twins are to go to the House of the Sacred Heart, an orphanage run by nuns.

Their mother is hysterical when we arrive, but she calms somewhat when Madame tells her what we intend to do. I gaze into the mother's tear-stained face. What if Sad Eyes had arrived before us? What if he'd … disposed of … the babies?

The father writes down the address of the orphanage on a scrap of paper. We tell them to memorize it, then tear up the page. At last we are out of there, and Madame and I carry the infants down the hill. With their small, starved faces, they look like kittens. My baby stares at me with milky-blue eyes that blink as the wind blows into them. His mouth is a tiny O and he is quiet for once, perhaps from the motion of walking. I want babies of my own after the war is over. I tell Madame. She snorts derisively.

"Nasty demanding things. Wouldn't want them around for more than a minute. Cat's bad enough."

She doesn't fool me for a minute. She adores them or wouldn't risk her life to save theirs. I think of my mother, how she ran upstairs and grabbed me before I fell out the window. We all want to rescue and cherish babies.

At the Sacred Heart, Madame orders me to hand my baby to her, then trundles them both inside, grumbling that they're heavy, that I should get lost, stop being a nuisance, go to work. Deeply hurt, I march down the road, the usual stupid tears stinging my eyelids and burning my cheeks. I helped save two lives today, and Madame didn't even thank me.

It isn't till much later that I realize why she acted that way: she didn't want me showing my face inside the orphanage or taking unnecessary risks. In her gruff fashion she's protecting me, like a mother.

It turns out to be a godsend.

Chapter Twenty-six

"All this stupid meddling," complains Sad Eyes. "Now look where it's got you." He has caught me at the factory during my lunch break and winds his hand around my arm, pulling me away from the other girls. Now he nags at me as I eat my sparse lunch of bread and turnip. I hate him watching while I eat. He has the emaciated appearance of an old, starving man, seems to count every crumb as it moves from my fingers to my lips.

"Where has it got me?" I offer him a piece of bread. He shakes his head too many times.

"Haven't got time to eat." Scratching his neck through his scarf, his long fingers bonier than ever, he's tense and exhausted. "Listen, Solange, the parents of those babies have been arrested. The Nazis found the address of the orphanage."

"Those poor people. We told them to tear up the paper." A huge lump of bread sits on my tongue, but I don't know whether to swallow or spit it out. "How do you know?"

"Madame Blanche got a message from the Mother Superior, her contact. She said the Gestapo were coming at seven tonight to pick up the twins."

Finally choking down the bread, I throw the rest on

the ground for the birds. With lightning speed Sad Eyes scoops it up and slams it into his mouth. I glance away. He really is starving.

"Well, we'll have to fetch the babies before seven, then," I say, taking care not to watch him chew.

"Not possible. The nuns don't want any trouble. They're afraid they'll be closed down."

Casually, I drop a slice of turnip on the seat beside us. When I look again, it's disappeared. I put another down.

"Those twins were meant to die, Solange."

He puts his hand on my arm again, but I shake it off and stand up abruptly.

Lunch break is over. A breeze is wafting the smell of new leather and boot polish at us. He's so certain of everything, there's really no point in my arguing. But fury is boiling up, threatening to suffocate me — the one who didn't want to help strangers, didn't want to get involved. "Isn't that typical? Mr. High and Mighty. Mr. Knows What to Do Every Single Time. No one can teach you anything, Mr. Fatalist."

He flinches. "I make choices, that's all. We have to sacrifice the few for the many ... or for the few. As long as *some* of us survive."

"Huh! It's that easy, is it?"

"It's not easy."

"But you'll make damn sure you're one of the survivors."

"I can't. There's too much chance involved."

Silence. Flies are buzzing. The wind has died. Beads of sweat break out across Sad Eyes' forehead and I feel grudgingly sorry for him.

"Listen," I say. "I have a great idea."

I speak low and fast, have just finished when Sad Eyes grabs me, throws both arms around me, and kisses me so deeply I can taste the food on his lips.

"Didn't realize it was that great an idea," I mumble, stunned.

I look up and see a soldier. I've not noticed him approach, could have given the whole game away.

"*Heil* Hitler." The soldier smiles. "Lovely to see young people in love."

"Spring fever, sir. Does things to a fellow." Sad Eyes kisses me again for good measure and strokes my face lovingly as the soldier goes on his way. "That was nice," Sad Eyes murmurs.

It *was* nice, or at least interesting, different from Walter's angel kisses, deeper and more insistent, even if only a ruse. But Sad Eyes still stands very close. His cheek is against mine, and I can feel the stubble of his beard, the pulse in his temple. I'm confused, move away and examine the cobbles.

Instantly, he is all business again, cracking his knuckles and grinning. "It's daring, but it might just work. I don't know if we should risk it, though."

"Please, Marcel," I beg. "I've held them. They're like my own babies. I can't just give up on them."

"Very well," he says, just like that. "We'll gamble." And slips away.

Chapter Twenty-seven

At 6:30 p.m., I'm standing just around the corner from the Sacred Heart. I'm wearing a dark jacket, dark skirt, dark hat, flat black shoes and a straight brown wig. A maroon slash of lipstick makes me appear older and more severe — I hope. Julie is with me, and my regular clothes are in her bag. In my pocket are documents confirming I'm a member of the Gestapo. A couple of boys from the Underground worked on them all afternoon.

"Lend me your eyeglasses, Julie. They'd look just right."

She peels them off and hands them over. A tiny girl with long, braided auburn hair, she has the innocent look of a young child. This is often quite useful to the Underground, but she makes me feel gigantic. Still, perhaps a fat black crow will make exactly the right impression.

"I can't see anything, Solange." She gazes at me myopically.

"I know. But you just need to stand here and wait, and I'll give your specs right back." Everything's blurred in the middle of the lenses, and my eyes keep darting sideways to see better. "Wish me luck."

"Luck."

In a moment I'm outside the front door of the orphanage. I slip into the vestibule, which, like my *Bubi*'s house, smells of wax and lavender. In front of me is another door, its top third a metal latticework.

"Yes?"

I jump. It's a nun, her face cut into lacy segments by the grille. I can hear children's laughter, the swish of a floor mop and the measured tick-tick-tock of a clock. Thank heavens I didn't come in here with Madame when she delivered the babies; I'd be recognized immediately. I really want to be elsewhere and my armpits are drenched. I pray the damp hasn't soaked through the jacket.

"*Heil* Hitler. I am here for the Jewish twins. Let me in immediately."

"I have to speak to the Mother Superior first."

"Let me in. The Führer's business waits on no one." I click my heels and salute, as I've seen Nazis do. That does the trick. A bolt slides back, and I'm escorted, with much bowing and scraping, to the Mother Superior, who greets me, rosary in hand.

"Captain Rosemarie Schultz. I've come for the Jewish infants." Clicking my heels again, I present my credentials, which she barely glances at. My hands are trembling badly. Afraid they'll give me away, I clasp them behind me.

"You're a little early." The Mother Superior is fingering her beads, her voice a whisper, her forehead set in a frown. She's more nervous than I am, which gives me a little courage.

"I have a great many things to do." I try to stare her straight in the eye but am half-blind. The spectacles were a ludicrous idea.

The nun hesitates. "Fräulein," she says, ignoring my rank, "couldn't you leave the babies here?"

"Fetch them at once."

"But Fraülein ... they have done no harm. Have a little compassion ... The Lord says ..."

"How dare you?" I scream, trying to re-create the ferocity of my fights with my mother. "Bring me the children before I have you all arrested." I'm terrified. The stupid clock is ticking away. The woman is getting on my nerves.

"They're only babies, Captain." She has remembered my rank. "And they're sleeping now."

She's weak, but I don't have the luxury of sympathy. I hit her hard across the face. My little finger catches her wimple, breaking my nail below the quick. Through the outer edge of the glasses I can make out the livid imprint of my palm and a slight bloody scratch on her cheek. She glares at me, enraged. My heart gallops with fear as her look of hatred stretches across two seconds, three, four. Then she collects herself, fingers her rosary and moves to the door.

"Get the twins," she tells someone outside. "Quickly. The Captain doesn't have all day."

In five minutes I'm out, a baby in each arm. As I speed around the corner, an enormous black car draws up at the orphanage. It's the Gestapo. I begin to shake violently; I don't think I can move. But four lives are at stake. I push myself toward Julie. She grabs a twin, tears the glasses off my face, hooks them over her ears and nudges me hard with her knee. Then she races off down the alley.

We'll be all right, I think. *We'll get the babies to the safe house.* My head woozy, my stomach trembling, I follow. We run frantically down side streets, ducking whenever we see a soldier or policeman. But her specs aren't anchored properly. Along the way they fly off, and before she can retrieve them I crunch them under my great, fat, Gestapo-shod feet.

Exhaustion has set in. My legs are about to explode, and my chest is so sore I can barely draw breath. I had pneumonia once, and this is exactly how it felt. Julie has been clinging to me for what seems like hours. Her bag bangs repeatedly against my thigh, and her arm is dragging me down.

"We have to stop a moment," I pant.

"Is it safe?"

"I don't care. Anyhow, I've got to change."

In a deeply recessed doorway, I slide out of the wig, Gestapo outfit and shoes and into my regular clothes while Julie shields me and holds both babies. Then I stuff the disguise into the bag — the Underground might need it again.

The twins are probably as numb and weary as I am. They are hardly making a sound, but their silence can't last long. Soon it'll be past time for a feed.

I take back a baby. "Which one are you?" I whisper. "Gaspard or Pierre?" There's no one left in the whole world who loves them enough to tell one from the other.

Julie's taken up the bag and gone ahead because we're so late. I can just see her in the dark, feeling her way along the wall. I follow as fast as I can. As I turn a corner I halt, dumbfounded. Blind as a bat, she's banged right into a soldier. His gun clatters to the ground, and he pauses to pick it up. *Get away, get away,* I think, but of course she can't. I shrink back into the shadows, covering my baby's mouth with my hand. We're much too close. I can see the lines under the soldier's eyes, his slight paunch. But he looks kindly enough.

"What do you do out so late, little girl? It's after curfew." He's mistaken her for a child. Good.

"My brother is sick, sir. My mother's away so I'm taking him to a friend to help him." That's the way of the Underground. You think fast or you die.

"He looks perfectly fine to me. We are searching for a girl who stole two Jewish babies from the nuns. What's in that bag?" He gestures toward it with his gun. I think I'm going to faint.

"Baby things, a bottle of milk."

Pulling the bag open, he lifts out my black hat and jacket and skirt and — the ultimate giveaway — the wig. He examines each garment meticulously before dropping it on the ground. The shoes are at the bottom. They fall to the pavement with ominous dull thuds.

"Let me see the baby."

"Please, sir, he's sick. And he doesn't take to strangers."

She doesn't move, so he takes the infant himself, unwrapping the little creature and inspecting him as thoroughly as the clothing. "It's amazing how Jewish babies look just like all the others," he says kindly, and my soul sparks with the tiniest flame of hope.

"Where's the other twin?" he asks.

"Twin?"

Singing a little, cradling the child in his arms, the soldier moves toward a tap set low in the wall of a house. He turns it on, a little awkwardly, with the hand that holds the gun. What can he possibly be doing? Does he mean to wash the baby? Baptize him? Gently, so gently, he holds the face of the child under the running water. "There you go, little baby," he croons in German. "Back to your Hebrew God." The infant cries once, tries to move his head to avoid the water, chokes, and is still.

I go limp with horror. Julie's screaming. "No, no, no."

Leaving the baby under the trickling tap, the Nazi asks, "So, where's the other twin?"

She's moaning quietly. One, two, three seconds tick by. Casually, he puts his revolver against her temple. "Sure you don't know?" She doesn't reply. Another second's pause. Then, as if it's the easiest thing in the world, he squeezes the trigger. He stares hard into the shadows, and I shrink back even farther. Then he strolls away.

Chapter Twenty-eight

Much later I drag myself toward home. Whatever befell the Grossman twins, or Eva and Manfred and Naomi, I didn't see — maybe nothing happened. Maybe they're still out there somewhere and I might meet them again. But Julie and the baby? I am a witness.

Sad Eyes pulls me into a doorway before I reach Madame's house. I don't even jump when he touches me. I'm too numb. It's almost dawn. Sad Eyes' face is ghost-like. "You can't go back there. It's not safe. You have to move on."

"What? Why?"

"The Gestapo arrested Madame Blanche. The Mother Superior must have told them where they could find her."

"Weak, stupid bitch."

"And they're probably searching for you."

I groan, almost falling against him.

"What happened?" he asks, putting a hand out to steady me.

"I got one of the babies to the safe house. He'll be shipped out to the country today. But the other baby's dead … Julie's dead." I sob quietly. "It's all my fault."

Horrified, Sad Eyes wraps his arms around me. As he hugs me, and I tell my story, my face brushes against the rough material of his jacket. I smell fear, his and mine. But he speaks firmly and gently. "No, it's not your fault. It's war. It's the way things are. You're a brave girl. If I'd thought of a better solution in the first place, none of this would have happened. But we do what we can."

"I need the cat." I can't bear to lose him, too. "Chandler, where is he? He has no one to look after him except me."

"He's fine. I saw him disappear behind the *charcuterie* a short time ago. Out for a meaty meal. We'll find him. Solange?"

"Yes?"

"I'm glad you're safe. You're very ... special ... to me."

I start to cry again. I don't know what to say. In the end, overwhelmed, I say nothing.

"I know there's someone else, Solange. Your eyes are even sadder than mine. Yes, Blanche told me what you call me. But I want you to ... be aware of how I feel."

"I'm aware," I whisper. "Amazed but aware. I have to go away now, don't I?"

"Yes, you do. You're burned as an operative in this area."

Chapter Twenty-nine

A new town. A new longer hair style, new name. But the same obstreperous three-legged cat, Chandler. Ungrateful he may be, but he's something to love. I hug him hard before he can escape. I talk to him, kiss his bullet head and stroke his poor, ragged stump. Usually he hisses, but the occasional purr is a delight. Chandler keeps me sane. Almost everyone I've ever known has died or disappeared, and on bad days I feel that it's my doing, that I bring terrible luck wherever I go.

Thanks to Sad Eyes' connections, I'm still working for the Underground. But it's my choice now. I do it because I need to — for vengeance? To keep me from despair? Who knows? I complete whatever task I'm set, grimly and quickly, and return to my damp little room and silence. There's no Madame Blanche here. No brusque but well-meaning words, or hats to borrow, or warm broth. No one but Chandler. In a way, it's best. It quiets my mind, deadens the ache. I don't want to climb inside anyone else's life anymore. I work, I eat when I can, I sleep. I no longer wonder when or if the war will end. Speculation is futile.

The only exception to my indifference is Walter, who lives in my dreams. Sad Eyes' kiss awakened me, but not to him. It's Elephant I want.

I've been helping move groups of Jewish children out of France: guides meet them at designated places and, for enormous sums, smuggle them through the German lines and into Switzerland. We pretend they're on school outings, and the subterfuge seems to work quite well. Ignoring their pitiful expressions and fierce need for love, I find them housing, help feed and ready them for exit. I am cold and efficient. "I've managed without my parents," I think, somewhat resentfully, "and so can you." Once I even smacked a little boy's hand off my arm. I can't risk that awful tug at the emotions, the way I did with the twin boys. It's too dangerous, leads to bad decisions. For me and for them.

I've just delivered a group of children to other operatives and am walking back to my room. There's bread in my bag, wine and a small treat for Chandler, begged from the butcher. The sun's behind me, the weather sultry. There's a slight breeze blowing, and for the first time in weeks I feel almost cheerful.

"Mouse." A single, faint word, in German, almost lost on the hot wind. My heart leaps in love and terror. The street's full of unfamiliar faces. No one looks at me. Nowadays people keep their eyes down, move swiftly, avoid involvement with strangers.

Have I imagined that voice because I want it so badly? I must be going mad. I must get home.

A quick movement. Someone is walking beside me with a fast, uneven step. The sun is burning into my back. The street smells of garbage and cabbage soup. A long thin shadow falls next to mine across the road. It's asymmetrical, stooped. Its owner has a faint limp. I can't bear to glance sideways.

"*Gott im Himmel*, I hardly recognized you. What on earth have you done to yourself? Your lovely, fine, mouse hair is all gone, run to dandelion seed."

I don't need to look.

He's in my room, sitting on the floor, stroking the cat. There is a salty smell to him, sweat and damp cotton and not enough soap. It is both familiar and strange, exciting. Chandler takes to him instantly, of course. That stupid ingrate of a cat hardly ever comes anywhere near me except to be fed.

"I've been going from one town to another for weeks, Mouse, trying to get across the border. It was hopeless, so I hiked here to try a different tack. When I saw you …"

"Yes?"

"Well, I couldn't believe my eyes." Moving to the bed, he kicks off his shoes. He is drinking wine out of a cracked cup. His long fingers are clasped tightly around the handle. I try not to look at the bloody marks where he's chewed his nails past the quick, concentrate instead on his dear, lean face, the miracle of having him there.

"Where are you staying?"

"Nowhere."

"Well, you can stay here tonight. You take the bed. I'll sleep on the chair."

"I can't believe I've found you, Mouse — I'd given up even looking. My one link to … everything."

After hastily swallowing some bread, he yawns and lies

down on his side. He has grown up, and I can't take my eyes off him. Awake, he intimidated me. I couldn't quite accept it was him. Dreaming, he is fragile, unattainable. I want to touch him, feel his heartbeat, know he's truly alive, but I don't have the courage. Instead, I cover him with my only blanket. It wakes him up.

"Mouse?" he murmurs sleepily.

"Yes, El?"

"Lie by me. I need your warmth."

Nervous, hardly daring to breathe, I creep in next to him. He turns and nuzzles against me, then, with an unfamiliar and unexpected gesture, tentatively touches my breast.

"Eleph," I whisper. "This is me. I'm not like all those pretty girls you always wanted. I'm just a mouse."

"Mouse is beautiful," he murmurs. "Elephant wouldn't change her for anything." He kisses me gently. I kiss him back, shower kisses all over his mouth and eyes — one tiny mouse kiss can't be worth much.

"I'm fat and lumpy," I say despairingly.

"You're not lumpy at all. You're big-boned and strong," he corrects me. "That's what's needed in a war." Thrilled, I almost expect him to say something else wonderful. Instead he is quiet.

"What are you thinking?" I ask after a minute.

"I'm only twenty-three out," he declares. I have no idea what he's talking about.

"Only twenty-three out, Mouse, in getting Hitler's name to add up to the number of the beast. I found a middle name for his grandmother, used that, did another few calculations ..."

He falls silent again. After a while he turns onto his back, throws his arms above his head on the pillow and goes to sleep. I stare into the darkness. Walter breathes softly, moaning a little. A tin can rolls down the road outside. Chandler purrs.

"I have Walter back, Cat," I whisper, with a fearful exultation. "He cares for me. Well, most of the time, when he's not preoccupied with other things. We must never lose each other again."

"For goodness' sake, stop fidgeting and mumbling, Mouse," Walter growls, turning away in a huff. "I'm trying to sleep."

"Should I get out of bed?" I blink back a tear.

"If you want to. Or just keep still and be quiet." Same old Walter.

The next morning, Walter's settled in. I know because he's busy with his bits of paper. Gematria. Kabbalah. Numbers, numbers, numbers. A frisson of fear runs along my spine, but it soon gives way to amused tolerance.

"Are you getting anywhere with it?"

"With what?"

"With your numerical plan to kill Hitler. Still twenty-three out?"

"Don't scoff, Mouse, please. It only shows your ignorance. Look at these figures." As he drags more scraps out of his pocket, the little card I gave him in La Blaize comes, too. So does the *Mogen David*, snaking to the floor and rolling off its broken chain. Chandler sniffs the chain, mews his

149

disgust and flounces away haughtily, as only a three-legged cat can flounce. No doubt he was hoping for a snack.

"You still have the *Mogen David*."

"My mother gave it to me." He's at work again and barely glances up.

"I'd like it back, please, Eleph."

"What?" He sounds profoundly irritated.

"The *Mogen David*. I'd like it back," I enunciate, very clearly and slowly. "I made a mistake out of anger when I threw it at you. I'm extremely sorry. Now I'd like it back."

"Sure. Anything else you want?" There isn't a scrap of grace to his giving.

"Not right now. I have to go to work."

He picks up the little card and stuffs it in his pocket. "Is there something for breakfast?"

"Not unless you go out and catch it."

"What?"

"You're not the only one working to defeat Hitler today. You expect me to make coffee and brioches?"

"Never mind." His lips are moving. He's adding. I could be on a different planet.

"Mouse is such a clever mouse," he whispered last night. "Elephant can't do without her." And "Mouse grows on you when you're not looking." ("Like fungus," I teased. We both laughed.) Just before dawn, he even murmured, "Elephant loves Mouse." Or at least, I'm pretty sure he did. Both of us were half asleep, snuggled under the blanket. Has he forgotten so soon? How typical.

I want us to be close, to talk. But he's gone into his own Walter-world of gematria, of dangerous calculations. They're clean, I suppose, less messy than feelings. Perhaps he feels safer that way, but somehow his withdrawing into his research only draws me closer.

I can't think about this anymore, I have to deliver some important papers. Besides, I suddenly understand that nothing will change him. If we stay together, I'll often feel put upon, frustrated, and madly in love, all at the same time.

"I do important work. The Underground may not be as important as gematria, but it's good enough for me."

He doesn't answer. His tawny head is now bent over a book — the mysteries of freemasonry. Chandler is curled on his knee, and Walter strokes him absently.

Hopeless. Both of them. Grabbing my hat, I fling the *Mogen David* in my pocket and bang out of the room. In the stairwell, I smile.

Although I'm unsure of his feelings for me, I can't get enough of his thin, bony frame, his light hair, his beautiful compliments when I catch him in the right mood. I gulp it all in because I can't believe anything will last. Even if we get through the war, there will be other problems. There always are.

Still, sometimes we're as close as it's possible to be; but it's not all peaceful: he makes impossible demands, goes behind his eyes where I can't reach him, and I counter by shouting or being sarcastic or slamming doors. I've even learned to laugh at him. He looks surprised, then annoyed, then usually laughs too.

"You're the glue that holds us together, Mouse," he

says. I can't help wondering whether he's happy about that. Maybe he's just here with me because all the other girls he's known have vanished. But I never have the courage to ask him. Maybe I don't want to know.

I can't stand the thought of his leaving, of being alone again. He still wants to go to Spain, but I'm committed to my work. Every package of papers delivered is a triumph, every child over the border a victory, small but significant.

When we discuss it, he blows up. He wants us safe, or at least away from the Nazis. And who can blame him? "Think of *us* for a moment, Mouse. You and me. We deserve to be out of all this."

I don't know how to reply, but I know I can't go. The thought of him leaving is cracking my heart open. I can't stand to have no one to hug me. Walter hugs me a lot. And kisses me. And lies in bed with his arm around me. I drag myself through each day, dreading his going.

"I can't leave you now, Mouse," he remarks one evening, to my astonishment. "We could get married after this damned war is over."

I stare at him incredulously. He's never mentioned marriage, and only talked of love that first night in bed.

"Wouldn't you want to get married?" He's plaintive.

"Want to? Eleph, we're too young — and this is not the time to think about it. But later ... do you really need to ask?"

"Good. That's settled."

"You make it sound like we've just decided what to cook for supper."

"Nonsense. Plans are plans. They have to be made objectively, not sentimentally."

"You're the most sentimental person I know. You even

kept the little card I gave you when I left La Blaize."

"Can't waste paper," he lies. "I have to be practical. Listen, now we've agreed to stay together, we have to find something for me to do. I can't keep Chandler company all day. Besides, he's lousy at numbers and chewed up my last two pencils."

We laugh. Chandler doesn't look a bit repentant.

"What do you want to do?"

"Same stuff as you, I guess." He sounds doubtful.

"There may be something in the Underground," I say slowly, unwilling to expose Walter to danger, but equally unwilling to decide his life for him. "Is that really what you want?"

"Of course. I want to … help you save people."

"If you're sure, I'll ask."

He thinks for a moment. "I'm sure."

I do, and there is work. He's not cut out to be a courier. He's too noticeable, too absent-minded. In any case, couriers are usually women. But after I vouch for him and we allow him to poke around, he soon finds a niche helping to forge papers in our small documents factory. It's the perfect job — why didn't I think of it? Extremely adept at detail, he wears small round spectacles that he's dug up on a market stall and peers at his work with an absorption he usually reserves for gematria or the Knights Templar. He looks like a baby owl, his arms flailing like wings when he can't get something right. The rest of us smile as though he's a small but brilliant child who needs to be humored.

I am suddenly at ease — he's safer in our hidey-hole of a factory than out on the streets.

For the moment he appears to be mine. So for the

moment, I'm happier than I've ever been.

One day I find a scrap of a journal he's keeping. Feeling a little ashamed, I begin to read his tiny, spidery writing, which slants upward and is hard to decipher. It's mostly about gematria, about the discoveries he's made and how close he is to defeating Hitler. But, "I'm afraid Mouse will abandon me," it says in German on the second-to-last page. "I'm not kind enough to her. But I'm not a strong person. And what do I have to offer?" I stare at the words till my tears make the letters dance. Put the journal down, dust around it carefully. Why did he leave it out like this? Forgetfulness, or did he mean me to see it? In any case, it's a revelation. I've always thought I was the vulnerable one.

Chapter Thirty

Sometimes the sounds of battle reach us, jagged booms that rattle the windows. It could be the British or the Maquis blowing up installations, but it's best not to ask. Perhaps because of this, the Nazis have grown much tougher. Swooping down, they check identification papers thoroughly and haul away anyone suspicious. I've even seen them pull down men's trousers to see if they were circumcised. Two were arrested. Appalled and frightened, humiliated for them, I pray nothing will happen while Walter and I are out together.

How things have changed. A boy's circumcision used to be a time for celebration. At my little brother's *bris,* the apartment was full of happy people, and Papa, flushed with pride, called out *"le chaim"* when the rabbi was done. Everyone drank wine, clinked glasses and ate the delicious little cakes Mama had been baking for days. I'd never seen so much food and stuffed myself with sweet yeast cakes until I had a bellyache. The rabbi, when he'd drunk too much wine, made a little joke. "I'm glad I didn't slip this time," he said. I didn't understand, but my uncle laughed his great rumbling laugh and dangled me from his arms so I could turn the special somersault he'd taught me.

"Your little brother didn't even cry. He's a proper Jew now, Esther," he said. "Say *mazel tov.*"

"*Mazel tov.*"

"There's my girl."

I crave that life now. It's all gone, swept away. Occasionally, it rides back on the giant wings of the memory birds. The wings whirr in my ears when I'm trying to sleep, but perhaps it's only the pounding of my heart. I am afraid for Walter, who lies next to me, and for myself. Scared we'll become only memories, too. I've stopped imagining happy endings. I don't cry. Ever. I seem to have no tears in me.

Wherever we go, he and I walk separately, several paces apart, so that if one of us is caught, the other can escape. If he were arrested, I'd not want my freedom, I'd want nothing. But he insists, says it's sound practice.

"There is an order to things," he insists, "and sound practice is part of that order." Sound practice must be his good-luck charm that will protect us from Hitler.

It's Sunday, although no church bells ring and even the birds are curiously silent. We are on our way to meet our group. We always take roundabout routes and meet in different places.

The day is oppressive, and a blanket of smoke or dirt hangs over the town, blocking out the blue of the sky. There's a terrible stench of sewers, as always in the humid weather. And, as always when I'm out on the street, my heart is clattering like a steam train. I walk sedately.

Walter is in a terrific mood; he was joking all morning at home.

"Why did Elephant pack his trunk?" he asked.

"Because he was going on a trip?"

"Because he had a nosebleed, silly Mouse."

I didn't understand the punch line, but I love him when he's like this. I want to be playful and link my arm in his. But of course it's not sound practice. He allows us to walk abreast for a minute, then pushes me ahead as we reach the more crowded streets. Still feeling playful, I slow down so we're together again. I grin at him coquettishly.

"Walk on, little Mouse." His lips are drawn in a tight line.

"You make it sound like I'm a horse."

"Walk on. That way I can keep an eye on you." His eyes are a dark gray today, almost gunmetal. There's no amber in them at all. He's lost every bit of humor.

"Plenty of me to keep an eye on," I joke.

"I like all of you. But not right now."

"El, it's such a lovely day. I just want us to forget the stupid war, to be together like any girlfriend and boyfriend."

"We're together every night."

"I want us to stroll together, like lovers in Paris."

He's getting really annoyed. "Walk on, little Mouse. Walk on, walk on."

I shrug as I usually do when he provokes me, and move ahead.

It is too quiet. Although there are at least twenty other people on the street, they are all silent, as though they're following a hearse. Nothing unusual, I tell myself. These are bad, bad times.

But a minute later, turning the corner, I'm confronted by Nazi soldiers. They're checking papers. It's too late to turn back without arousing suspicion, and much too late to warn Walter, so I stroll past them nonchalantly, swishing my skirt and smiling. I've painted black lines up my legs to look like stocking seams, and I show them off as I hike my skirt. The soldiers smile back. One whistles.

"I like curvy girls," he calls.

"Pig," I murmur, as I mock curtsy.

Walter is still behind me, so close I hear him mutter something, can almost feel him breathing down my neck. Another few steps and we'll both be out of danger. But like walking a tightrope across a raging torrent, our parade past the soldiers seems to go on forever. The camaraderie is gone. *God, please get us through this. Keep Walter safe and I'll do anything you want.*

"Halt."

I jump, but keep going. Best to seem unconcerned. Perhaps he's not talking to me.

"Halt. That girl there in the flowered skirt. The man in the shirtsleeves. Halt or I'll shoot."

I stop and turn slowly. The sun is burning the top of my head. An old woman across the street is gesturing at me with her umbrella. The stench of drains is overpowering.

A soldier stands between Walter and me, pointing to the ground. "Whose is this?" he screeches.

What's he glaring at? A child screams far off, and I'm distracted for a moment. Then I catch the gleam of gold. God in Heaven. It's the *Mogen David.* I stare at it in horrified awe.

"Whose is it?" the soldier screams again. I say nothing. Bits of my life are untangling from my brain and flashing in front of me. I shift from one foot to the other, uncertain, terrified. This is the moment I've always dreaded. I always knew it would come. I stare down at the *Mogen David*. The damn thing must have fallen from my pocket when I curtsied. Why must I be so clever? Why must I carry it with me everywhere? How can I be so stupid? Walter has warned me countless times, but the little extension of him is too precious to leave in our room. I'm going to die today.

"It's yours, isn't it?" the Nazi demands, glowering at me. The meaning of my entire life is concentrated in this instant. I need to be brave, own up, to save Walter. And I must be fast.

But the thought of death is overwhelming, and Walter is faster. "False hypothesis." He winks at the soldier. "It's mine. It belonged to my mother. I must have dropped it. *Heil* Hitler." He says all this in German, jerking his arm forward in an insulting parody of a salute, then, as an encore, reaches into his pocket, pulls out pieces of paper covered in Hebrew writing and lobs them into the air. They float to the ground like confetti.

"*Gott im Himmel.* I'm the Yid son of a bitch you're looking for. You're really slow on the uptake. The Führer should put you in his little black book." Walter grins. Then, "Hickory dickory dock," he singsongs in English, which we're both learning. "The mouse ran up the clock. Run up the clock, little mouse, and be quick about it, before it strikes one."

"Arrest the Jew," screams the soldier.

Arrest the Jew. Arrest the Jew. Walter is still grinning, a hard miserable grin. People on the street are gaping, as if they're at a sideshow. I feel horribly dizzy, want to yell, shriek, cry out, but his eyes are ordering me to stay silent. The soldiers punch him in the stomach, drag him away, throw him into a waiting truck, but he stares at me the whole way. His eyes are fire. They burn hotter than the sun. The truck drives off. My life breaks inside me.

"What are you staring at, girl?" a soldier hisses.

"Nothing, nothing at all." My voice isn't mine, it belongs to someone else. My head feels as if someone's stabbed me over and over in the neck. I try to concentrate on the pain. It stops me from thinking about Walter's bravery and my silent, cowardly betrayal of him.

"Do you know the Jew?"

"Know him? Of course not. What do you take me for?" There. I've betrayed him again.

I bite my upper lip, put one foot in front of the other, walk. Suddenly, on rounding the corner, I get Walter's elephant joke and I howl with laughter. I laugh and laugh till my laughter turns to hard, choking sobs that rake my lungs. Soon I'm doubled over against a wall, crying and gasping. People are staring. The sun has disappeared. The street stinks of death. I have to get out of here before I scream and am arrested or shot. I've forgotten where I'm supposed to be going, but a small voice sings in my head. "Walk on, little Mouse. Walk on, walk on."

When I get home, I don't know what to do with myself — stand up, sit down, stride around the room. My mind is racing, clacking on and on and I can't make it shut up. I want someone, anyone, to stop me. I want to be swaddled in a big warm blanket. A warm white sheet with satin seams, like in the old days. So my arms and legs won't move. So my brain goes blank. So I can be a child again. So someone else can take responsibility. Please. Please. I feel full and empty, raging and hopeless. The cat jumps out of my way with a yowl. Someone upstairs bangs on the floor. I want to cry but can't.

Why was I silent when they took him? Why didn't I scream at the soldiers, hit them, kick them? How could I have given Walter such treachery in return for his love? What's the worst thing that could have happened? I could have died — *I could have died* — and I protected myself from that. I'm not like Mama. I didn't run after the truck yelling at the driver, as she did when they took Papa away. Even poor Mama was braver than I am. Everyone in the world is braver than I am. The idea of death is so terrifying I can't face it.

Near evening, I slow down but am still restless. In a belated and futile show of courage, I go back to the scene after curfew, moving cautiously from one pool of shadow to another. The *Mogen David* is still there, though someone's kicked it into the gutter. Making sure no one's watching, I pick it up, kiss it, and shove it into my pocket. It's a last, glittering piece of Walter.

I go home and wait, as if he'll return. I sit, hour after hour, staring at the door. I cross my arms one way, then the other way.

"It was all a mistake, Mouse," he'll say. "Here I am, come safely back to you."

I put the little star on top of his journal, arrange his few clothes into a neat pile. He will come back. He will come. He will.

I sit down and cross my arms again, so my fingers hug my elbows.

But no one comes except a member of the Jewish Underground, scratching on the door late at night to see why we didn't meet the others as planned. My arms ache, I tell him. They've been in the same position too long.

Three weeks later, a dog-eared card arrives in the mail:

In the event of an accident, call Mouse.
Remember this card, Mouse?
I'm on a train headed east. I'll throw this out the window with your address on it, and perhaps some kind soul will mail it to you. Good luck, stay alive, God bless you and keep you. Love you always and forever, my darling Mouse. No one has ever been as kind to me as you.

El

Now I cry.

Chapter Thirty-one

Sad Eyes comes from miles away to visit. There's rain on his boots. Chandler licks it off.

"I heard you were unwell."

"Yes." I wish he'd go away.

"Things have been hard for you. You've lost the someone who is special?"

"Yes."

"He might survive. Even in a camp."

"Ha."

"You can never be sure." He tugs at his scarf. "God moves in mysterious ways."

Others have said the same stupid things. They should be ashamed to talk such rubbish.

"Anyway, I came to tell you we might be able to get you out. Over the mountains, through Andorra, into Spain."

"I don't want to get out."

"Listen, Solange, if you're going to stay, you must start caring again."

"My name isn't Solange. It hasn't been for ages."

"You have to stop all this self-pity. You're not the only one suffering. Last week we lost an entire convoy of children and Marianne, our operative. They were all arrested. Marianne's dead — hacked to death with an ax."

I'm furious. "Why are you telling me this? To make me feel even more guilty? Doesn't it occur to you I feel bad enough already?"

"Sorry. That was stupid of me." He stays a little longer. "If there's anything you want ..."

"There isn't."

"If you change your mind ..."

"I'll get in touch. Thank you."

He leaves. I feel a creepy pleasure at having rattled him.

Chapter Thirty-two

A church with a tall tower stands on the other side of town. I've often glanced at it as I passed. It's amazing to me that, no matter what happens, no matter what atrocities are committed, people still flock to it — still put their faith in God — and the door's always open, as if waiting for them. The church's stone changes color depending on the weather and the time of day. Late in the afternoon, it's a pinkish purple, like the rhododendrons in Berlin. I've scarcely been out in weeks. Why have I come here now?

Inside, unfamiliar odors greet me: incense, ancient chill, stale air. Sitting in a pew, I gaze around. Ahead of me sit women in dark headscarves. My head is bare. I'm not used to churches, feel out of place, recognizable. But no one looks at me. A sour-faced priest goes about his business in front of an enormous crucifix and stained-glass windows with their rainbow prisms of glass. Everything in the gloom is alien, moldy smelling.

It's so different from our little synagogue at home. On the women's side, everyone chattered, though the beadle would shush them and purse his lips. The smell of bread, baked by my father on Friday for the after-service *kiddush,* and left to warm on a radiator, wafted over the congregation. I re-create that scent in my mind. My mouth waters, but those days will never come again. There is a thresh of wings, and I look up, perhaps anticipating angels. A trapped bird skids and swoops around the vaulted ceiling. What am I doing here?

I make my way through a small door with a sign: *To the Tower*. Well-worn stone steps lead up and out of sight; all is evil-smelling and musty. I begin to climb although I have no idea why. The spiral staircase is narrow, and as I ascend I meet only a young boy coming down. It's a tight squeeze, but I hug the wall and we manage to pass each other.

"There's no heaven up there, high as it is," he grins. I don't respond but continue to climb until my legs ache. Just when I'm about to give up, I reach and pass through another door onto a small landing. Light streams through an archway, and I make my way over to it, gaze down at the town.

Now I know why I'm here. The buildings appear far away, unreal, lit by sun and turning their roofs, like flower faces, to the sky. I want to float, suspended in air, forget. Closing my eyes, I imagine I'm the red-and-green kite I had as a small child. In my memory, it is still adrift on the wind.

Grasping the ledge, I pull myself up until I'm framed in the Gothic arch. I spread my arms, feel the cold breeze on my face — and am seized from behind.

"No you don't." A man's voice, warm and low pitched.

Doesn't he understand? I need to fly. I kick at him and scratch his hands, but he doesn't let go.

"I'm a kite," I complain, as if that explains everything.

"No, you're not. You're a strong, healthy girl, and you'll plunge to earth like lead."

"Can I never jump out of windows," I yell, "without someone trying to stop me?"

"I don't know. How often have you tried?" He lifts me down, still kicking and scratching.

I lean my head against the ledge. "Why can't everyone leave me alone? What is it with all you do-gooders?"

"Listen, things may seem terrible now —"

"What do you know?" I ask nastily.

It's as if I haven't spoken. "— but one day the war will be over and you'll build a new life."

"This has nothing to do with the war." How can he be so stupid?

"Whatever it is, you have to hang on."

"All very well for you to say. I betrayed a friend, denied knowing him. Now he's probably dead. There's no new life after that." I begin to cry, thinking of Walter, his thin, dear body and what the bastards have done to it.

"So it is to do with the war. Peter denied knowing Jesus three times before the cock crowed, to save his own skin. Yet the church made Peter a saint. Everyone betrays someone in war."

"What the hell do you know about it?" Angrily, I spin around. In front of me stands a Nazi soldier: uniform, swastika, medals, everything. Suddenly I realize we've been speaking German — the forbidden language, the language that says I am not Nicole, not Solange, but Esther. It lies, like rotting meat, on my tongue.

"I'm a Jew," I yell, spitting a great gob of saliva into his face. "Now I've given you provocation. Shoot me."

Shocked at the attack, his hands ball into fists. He glares, his pupils large and black, and makes a slight move toward his gun. There's a ghastly pause as my spit drips slowly down his cheek.

Finally, I understand he might do something dreadful. Permanent. Suddenly I no longer want that. *The worst thing that could happen is that I could die,* I tell myself, and the thought is still as terrible as it was the day they took Walter away.

The spell is broken. "Don't be silly," the soldier says, wiping off the saliva and grabbing me by the shoulders. "Shooting you would make a mess in this holy place. And anyway, you weren't meant to die today."

Still terrorized, I say nothing.

He shakes me. "Didn't you hear me? You weren't meant to die today. If you had been, God wouldn't have put me in your way. He'd have sent the Gestapo."

His eyes are such a light blue I seem to see right through to his brain. I don't visualize blood. I imagine cogs and wheels, clean, glittering, running smoothly. For some reason this calms me.

He drops his hands, stands more upright. "I've a daughter of around your age."

I want to stay silent but cannot. "What's that to me?"

"She reminds me that your life is valuable. Look, we're all in this together."

"Right," I sneer, getting angry again. "Except you're the hunter and I'm the hunted. And there aren't any rules."

"Soldiers do not squander life," he says thoughtfully.

"Ha! Look around you. What else is there here but squandered life?" I reply, thinking of Walter again.

"You are right. Butchers have wasted lives and *materiel* on senseless schemes that have led nowhere. Pointless, self-indulgent."

Am I beginning to understand this soldier? Does he have his own version of Sad Eyes' ethics of necessity? For him, it seems that killing Jews is wrong because it is unnecessary, not good soldiering.

"Most of us just want to get back to our families," he goes on. "Finish this stupid, wasteful war. And forget."

"That's what I wanted to do when I came here, too — forget. You haven't let me."

He pauses again, looks through the arches at the town. His eyes soften.

"That's because you chose a very permanent way to go about it, my dear." Now he actually smiles. He looks and sounds like my uncle in Berlin, smells like him, too, like the shaving soap he used.

Danger past, I start to cry again. "There's nothing left for me," I gulp. "And ... and ... I can't get down the stairs." God, I hate myself for sounding so pathetic. "My legs are too shaky from the climb. And I have to feed my cat."

"So there is something left for you. I'll help you down. If we see anyone on the steps we'll separate. But please humor me — don't try to jump out of this window for at least a month."

"I'll be too tired to climb up again. How many stairs are there anyway?" I grumble, as we go through the door.

"A hundred and fifty-four. I climb them once a month. Twice the number the faithful man must climb to reach heaven."

Gott im Himmel. A Nazi soldier who would get on famously with Walter.

Chapter Thirty-three

On my way home, I argue back and forth with myself about what's best to do. Crossing herself and muttering a prayer, an old woman gives me a wide berth. She clearly thinks I'm mad. Perhaps I am. I'm also totally exhausted, with blisters starting on my heels from all the stairs, and a filthy taste in my mouth.

Chandler greets me by rubbing between and around my ankles, and I feed him some scraps. Then I go to bed for three days, getting up only to pee or get a drink. Good God, even I must be losing weight. But it doesn't matter any more, has nothing to do with who I might be. On the fourth morning, I fill a bowl with water and wash myself thoroughly. Then I dress and write a letter. It takes me a very long time.

Dearest Sad Eyes,

I should say Marcel, I know, but when I imagine your dark, haunting eyes it seems as if I'm speaking directly to you.

I'm sorry for the way I behaved last week. You're right, of course — too much self-pity. And you were right about something else, too, some time ago. As long as some of us survive this war, we've won. It's a hard thought, but it's true. It might not be me, it might not be you, and it certainly won't be Walter; but still, we can work to save as many of us as possible. If one Jew survives, Hitler has failed.

I used to ask myself: What's the worst thing that could happen? My answer was always that I might die. Well, it's still the worst thing that might happen, but now, maybe, I can shrug and carry on. Oh, I'm still afraid, but in a sad kind of way I'm getting used to the idea. It's become part of my thinking. Everyone dies sooner or later, and I've seen a lot of death lately. I wanted to be immune to it, but I can't be. Still, I can't let worrying about it paralyze me. I'll go back to the Underground in a week or so. Maybe I could replace Marianne. I'd even take a gun and fight, like girls in the Maquis. Of course, I'll do whatever they need me to. (I'll give this letter to a courier here, so eventually it'll make its way to you.)

My friend Walter said something important, before he was arrested. He said I wasn't lumpy and fat. I was big-boned and strong, and that was what was needed in a war. I'm still very sad, always will be, I think, but I must use the strength God has given me. I must learn to rely on myself.

I'm grateful for your friendship. God bless and keep you.

Next year in a new, free France!

I don't know how to sign the letter. Who am I, anyway? Now Esther is gone, along with Nicole, Solange — and Mouse. Today I have a floating identity, tomorrow I'll be someone new. It doesn't really matter. Sad Eyes will know who the note is from — the inner person who is me will always be me.

I put the note aside and go to the shelf, where the *Mogen David* lies on Walter's journal. I should hide it. I should hide the journal, too, if I want to stay alive long enough to do some good and ease my guilt. But they comfort me, as do his threadbare clothes. I can still faintly smell Walter on them.

But it's the *Mogen David* that somehow contains his essence. There is a tiny sensation of evil when I touch it. Unintentionally, it helped me betray him. But there's great good in it, too. It reminds me of how he cared for me, how he valued my life above his own. Very softly I lay it across my palm. It has passed from his mother to him to me. Who had it before his mother? And who will have it after me?

It cannot be owned. It is on loan. A small gold star. Six Hebrew points. A broken filigree chain. They glisten.

Acknowledgments

The Thought of High Windows is a work of fiction. The characters, whether good or bad, kind or nasty, are entirely fictitious, figments of my own imagination. They speak in my mind, but have never spoken in the real world. I'd like to emphasize that from the outset.

However, the idea for the book came originally from a true story, the story of a hundred children who escaped Germany and Austria just before the second world war and moved first to Belgium, and then to France, to live in a castle called Château La Hille under the shadow of the Vichy government and the Nazis.

I borrowed the story and made it my own, and although Esther and Walter never existed, some of their brave exploits, and the exploits of other characters, did occur, although somewhat differently from the way I have portrayed them here.

I'd especially like to thank Walter Reed, one of the children of La Hille, for being my "contact," answering my interminable questions, and in general being so helpful to me. Another La Hille child, Ruth Usrad, wrote a work of nonfiction in Hebrew titled *Entrapped Adolescence*. Ruth was kind enough to allow me to borrow some of her very brave adventures, mentioned in her book, and pin them on my characters. Edith Goldapper was also kind enough to allow me access to her unpublished diary of the time, which helped me fill in details of everyday life. Inge Vogelstein pointed me toward some of her reminiscences on the internet. Joseph Dortort, another La Hille survivor, sent me photographs of his childhood, and of his time at La Hille and afterward. He asked me to look at them and "make up [my] own story." This I did. Thank you all. Your courage was and is awe-inspiring. And thanks to the many other men and women, survivors of La Hille, of Le Vernet, and of the second world war, who helped in one way or another to fashion the story.

I'd like also to extend my thanks to the Toronto Arts Council and the Ontario Arts Council. Their generous grants gave me the time necessary to complete the book.

To Barbara MacDougall, for her help in translating source material; to Chandler, of David Mason Books, for allowing me to use him as a character; to Michael and all my friends and family who've helped — you know who you are — thanks a million.

Thank you Valerie Hussey of Kids Can, and all the people who work there, for believing this was a worthwhile story to tell. Thank you, too, Leona Trainer. No one has ever had a better agent. You have been a close friend and an invaluable support during the writing of the book and various trials and tribulations. And finally, a big thank you to Charis Wahl, my editor and friend. It has been such a pleasure working with you, and a true learning experience. I can't imagine how I would have managed without your incredible expertise and assistance.

About the Author

Lynne Kositsky has degrees in psychology, education and English, and has been a middle school, secondary school and university teacher. She has won the prestigious E.J. Pratt Medal and Award for poetry and an international White Raven Award, given by the International Youth Library in Munich to books that "contribute to an international understanding of a culture and people." She lives in Toronto with her husband, son and two shelties.